STO

RANGER
IN SKIRTS

by Shirley Sargent

Nashville   ABINGDON PRESS   New York

1437194

This book is dedicated with appreciation and gratitude to the fine staff of ranger-naturalists, both permanent and seasonal, who make Yosemite National Park more meaningful to its many visiting owners—the people of the United States.

While the Yosemite places described in this story are real and the activities led by ranger-naturalists valid, all of the events and characters are wholly imaginary.

CHAPTER I

"Entering Yosemite National Park," read the wood, roughhewn sign. To Molly Bishop, the carved words said "heaven on earth." At the first turnout she nosed her car off the highway, parked, and climbed joyfully into a world fragrant with pine needles and blooming wild flowers. Swiftly she walked to the edge of a bank to look at the greenness of massed pines, oaks, manzanita bushes, and spring grass. She shoved auburn hair off her high forehead, straightened her tall, trim figure, and was warmed by the sun, the forest outlook, and the knowledge that Yosemite National Park was to be her home for the summer.

Her hair was tangled, her lipstick worn off, and her tortoise-shell glasses askew. Yet her lively, freckled face showed shy beauty.

Working with children in Yosemite Valley had been her idea of heaven ever since Yosemite's Chief Park Naturalist had lectured to her University of Southern

California geology class. Afterwards she had lingered with a group of other appreciative science students; shyness keeping her from congratulating him on his absorbing talk.

Dale Hudson's rumbling voice had fitted the big, green-uniformed, six-foot-two form. "I have a postscript for you cliff dwellers," he had said. "As you may know, Yosemite's summer ranger-naturalist staff is beefed up with the addition of various teachers in the science field. These men guide hikes and bird walks, give talks, answer questions, and interpret the natural wonders to Park visitors. We still have an opening this summer."

Feet shifted. Molly visualized Yosemite Valley, the geological marvel. With her family she had visited there, staying in a swank hotel, touring in sight-seeing buses.

"But," the ranger smiled, "your bright-eyed, eager expressions will fade when I add, this person needs to be a biology major with experience in botany and zoology."

Molly thought of her high school and college years immersed in those sciences.

The ranger continued, "And have had considerable experience with children in nature study, preferably in a summer camp environment. This requisite is because our weekday Junior Ranger program demands understanding of children as well as plants and animals."

Molly sighed, wishing for the ten thousandth time that she had been born a boy. The job suited her abilities and passions, but not her sex.

"The pay is small," Ranger Hudson smiled. "The board is a shared housekeeping tent in Camp 19, the ranger-naturalists' camp, where children outnumber the jays; but the surroundings and interpretive opportunities are unequaled. Any candidates listening?"

The geology professor asked, "Men only?"

"No. Yosemite has had several women ranger-naturalists in the past few years. Do you have someone in mind?"

"Yes, Molly Bishop. You have described her to a T. Molly, come on up."

Hesitantly she complied, scarcely daring to hope. The other students drifted away as the geology prof introduced her, culminating, "Molly's grown up in a Los Angeles apartment, yet she has a knowledge of the outdoors seldom rivaled by a country girl."

"How was that accomplished?" the ranger questioned skeptically.

"By tagging after the gardener, and spending full summers since I was six at a mountain camp."

"Any nature experience as a counselor?"

"Yes, three years."

"Doing what? Nature walks?"

She answered his sharp questions for over half an hour, forgetting her natural timidity to describe group experiments in cooking bulbs, making track casts, and recognizing bird calls. Warmth and enthusiasm colored her voice and hazel eyes.

Finally, the ranger shook her hand and said pleasantly, "If you will complete this application form and send it up, pass a physical, and satisfy a few other details, I think you have a summer job. Can you report for training session June sixteenth?"

That would be the Monday after USC was out, she

calculated, nodding vigorously, mentally making plans.

"Fine. I'll be sending you informational pamphlets on natural and historic features of Yosemite plus specifications on the women's uniform. Prices and addresses are included in the material, and you should order soon.

"Yosemite will have two rangers in skirts this season. You two will share a tent with our museum curator. Your main duty will be the Junior Ranger program for young visitors eight to thirteen years old, but you will have other jobs, and campfire talks."

"Talks?" Molly tensed. "To adults?"

"Yes, but with their many, many children."

She swallowed. "I'm not much on public speaking. People *en masse* unnerve me."

"Me too, but half of our summer Yosemite audience are children. Just speak as you have to me and you will be fine."

Later, Molly remembered, there had been explanations to, and protests from, her mother, father, and teenage sister, Carol.

Molly had told them, confidently, "In Yosemite most of my work will be with children. The naturalist staff runs a Junior Ranger nature center five mornings a week with one all-day hike. I'm to teach youngsters about mammals, birds, geology, Indians—all the things I like."

"Ugh." Carol dismissed the job with a shrug. "Outdoorsy things! 'Roughing it' in our apartment suits me."

Mr. Bishop's dark eyes twinkled. "Molly, your room is a jungle of butterfly nets, microscopes, and pine cones. This job sounds like a natural, though I hope you will have some work with adults. Your shyness, with anyone beyond the freckles and black eye set, worries all of us."

Molly reddened. "It shouldn't. After college graduation, I'm going to teach high school science, and be a happy old maid. Anyway, Dad, the naturalist who hired me said something ominous about museum lectures and campfire programs."

"There will be lots of children at both to comfort you," her mother remarked drily. "At least, it won't be a summer camp atmosphere with *everything* geared to youngsters. We want you to grow up."

Molly said hotly, "Don't forget I am almost twenty, almost a college senior. I drive a car, earn money, have a checking account. . . ."

"Live at home," he interceded smoothly, "rarely date, do nothing social, avoid campus activities, and hide from anyone over sixteen."

Molly blushed, knowing he was right. Her interests were so different from other students, she found it hard to talk to her own age group. It was impossible to communicate with her parents' friends who talked of bridge, politics, and club work. Her shyness, independence, and passion for the outdoors tongue-tied her except with children, with whom she was perfectly at ease.

Mr. Bishop had rumpled Molly's hair. "Don't scowl so. I do want you to mature socially, but you are my favorite older daughter."

Mature socially! Molly frowned and picked up a pine cone, examined it absently, and dismissed her father's words. A glance at her watch hurried her back to the car.

It was already two o'clock, and she had written the Park personnel that she would arrive in Camp 19 at two. If she drove straight there, she could make it by three.

But it was after seven before she drove her packed car into the parking area in front of Camp 19, and surveyed it excitedly. Tents, half-hidden by woods and blooming azalea bushes, faced her in a semicircle backed by rocky slopes. A stone's throw from behind the car, across the highway, the Merced River lazed.

Instead of heading toward the nearest tent for instructions, Molly walked to the river. The evening sun muted forest colors of blue and green. The river itself was deep, deep green, and quiet except for wild splashing at the edge by a boy.

"Mother said no swimming, Foxy," an older girl tugged at his arm. "Come on. We promised to come straight back to camp."

"I'm not swimming; I'm wading, and I was skipping rocks until you grabbed me. I'll come in a minute." He glared ferociously. "Can't a guy ever be alone?"

Molly's heart was touched by his lament. She studied him sympathetically as the girl stomped off. He looked about eleven, gap-toothed, freckled-faced, and stubby-haired. He was dressed Sunday fashion with a white shirt, cords rolled up to his knees, and discarded Oxford shoes above him on the bank. Campers, Molly surmised, just arrived. Probably he needed, as she did, to be away from cars, noise, and people.

She slipped her sandals off, and waded in downriver so as not to intrude, shivering convulsively, happily, as her toes curled under the icy, snow-fed water. Golden

10

insects whirled in the last rays of the sun; Half Dome's bald top was sunlit, and still snow-mantled.

She envisioned the Merced River as a snake that threaded its lazy way down the seven-mile-long, glacial-gouged valley, remembering that its width varied from a quarter of a mile to a mile at its widest part. Over the Valley's three-thousand-foot granite walls crashed numerous snow-fed waterfalls. In the distance, she heard the booming of spectacular Yosemite Falls.

Molly skipped a rock across the river's placid surface. Although the Valley's altitude was 3,900 feet, she felt higher than Half Dome's 7,531-foot height.

Before the summer was over, she promised herself, she would hike Half Dome, and explore many of the trails and peaks included in Yosemite's 760,000 acres.

Her expert stone-skipping attracted the boy to her side. He watched silently, blue eyes alive with wonder. Still silent, she showed him how by picking small, flat rocks for him and guiding his arm. After splashing them for a while, he skimmed a rock across the river surface a spatterless fifty feet. He grinned up at her delightedly, and she clapped a congratulatory hand on his shoulder.

A loud voice startled them. "What are you doing in the river, Brewster? Why didn't you come back half an hour ago?"

The boy looked to Molly, his eyes imploring. "It's partly my fault." She faced the scowling man. "I was teaching him how to skip rocks."

"Can't you see it's growing dark?" Abruptly, the man calmed. "Sorry, in the light I thought you were younger than you are. Brewster isn't a good swimmer so his mother and I worry when he's off alone. You do understand."

His manner was smooth and apologetic, but Molly resented his intrusion and close scrutiny of her. His face was florid and moonlike under an iron-gray butch haircut; his blue eyes measuring and curious.

"If you have lost your way, the public campground's on up the river."

Molly shook her head, pointing. "I'm staying at Camp 19, across the road."

"You are?" The boy's voice was joyful. "We are too."

"Are you Molly Bishop?" The man sounded almost displeased, though his tone was hearty. "Headquarters told me you were expected this afternoon. Why haven't you reported in? I'm Ranger-Naturalist Breckenridge Fox, sort of the camp 'father,' and I have been waiting for you to show up."

Molly shook hands, thinking, grimly, that her mother would be pleased at the chaperonage of a camp "father."

Just as her hand was swallowed in his grasp, so was her independence during the next two hours.

"Camp 19 is a friendly place," he explained. "We all go by first names—just call me Breck—and have lots of sociability, especially at nights after campfire talks."

Molly listened, dismayed at the togetherness he spoke of as seemingly integral to a naturalist's life.

"We criticize each other's talks and do everything possible to see that our services make Park visitors' stays more meaningful." His round face was earnest. "You might say I'm the unofficial mayor of this camp. My wife Betty and I have been here three summers, and we help settle problems, give advice, and guide seasonal rangers so that we have a happy camp. Now, come along and meet the other naturalists."

Molly met ten men, their wives, and a small army of mosquito-bitten children. Breck Fox piloted her around the tents, the large washhouse with showers, toilets, two washing machines, and a walk-in refrigerator.

"We call this the bear baffle," he laughed, "because everyone keeps food perishables here away from hungry bears. Each tent has an ice cupboard in there. Are you afraid of bears?"

"No, but I have great respect for them." Molly remembered times she had chased bears off in the mountains by banging on pans, shouting, and shining lights.

"Good. I'm glad you are not timid, but, remember, anytime you have a fear or a problem, just come to our tent. Betty and I have coffee, counsel, and cheer to offer at all times."

Molly could not escape his overbearing kindness or his insistence that she have dinner with his family. The meal was large; the Foxes vocal, and smothering to her.

Betty Fox explained the housekeeping setup. "Each tent is really two, with cement floors and screened sides. In the front room, like this, is a sink with cold running water, a table, cupboards, and a wood cookstove. The back tent is for sleeping quarters." She sighed. "That's the bad part—five of us in a 12 by 14 space. Of course there will only be three girls in your tent when the others arrive."

Mentally Molly recoiled at the idea of sharing a tent with two perfect strangers. At home, she had had a bedroom to herself always and, even at camp, a place outside, apart from her charges. "I'll sleep outside," she announced quietly, "so I won't bother the others if I snore."

Breck Fox boomed positively, "Sleeping outdoors isn't a good idea at all. Those broken talus slopes back of camp host all sorts of animals, including rattlesnakes. So long as I'm responsible for the well-being of this camp, I don't like anyone sleeping outside."

Molly was still, wanting to escape to her tent, but he insisted on helping to carry things in from her car.

Finally he suggested, "This tent is off by itself so that, until your tentmates come, perhaps you had better bunk with us, in the front room as it were."

Molly gulped and steeled herself inwardly against the domineering man who somehow represented all she disliked and feared about people.

"Thanks, Mr. Fox," she said stiffly, "for the offer and all your kindness tonight, but don't worry about me. I'm quite independent and capable after thirteen full summers of camp, three of them as a counselor."

"Well, well," he remarked, taken back at her declaration of independence. "You are a hog on ice, aren't you? That's fine. I admire a girl with spirit; but remember, to have a happy camp, there has to be give and take, cooperation from everyone. I'm sure you understand that after all your camp experience. Good night."

Molly watched him go, realizing she had antagonized him and not really caring, so long as he left her alone. She unpacked quickly, sleeping bag, clothes, cooking supplies, and her nature equipment. Her plant press, microscope, nature books, and miscellaneous apparatus took up one corner of the front tent. She hoped her tent mates wouldn't mind. The community living frightened her. Tentmates, one central washhouse, and walk-in refrigerator meant a necessarily social, interdependent camp. She had not expected regimentation.

Iron cots stood in each corner of the sleeping tent. There was one scarred chest and a makeshift closet. The canvas was rolled up to let in fresh air. To her, one intangible, loved aspect of mountain living was sleeping outdoors under the stars. Inside here, she would face tentmates who might object to the canvas flap being up; outside, perhaps a nocturnal bear or raccoon.

Too keyed up for sleep, she drew on a jacket, and skirted the lighted parking lot for a path by the river. The night was moonless, but star-shot. Their glittering was mirrored in the dark, serpentine river. She welcomed the forest peace, the coldness that made her skin prickle, the loved, long-familiar night sounds—a plaintive owl, the sighing breeze, a ground-thudding pinecone.

These sounds had a new immensity and mystery in the glacial valley whose age and aloofness impressed her. Camp 19 seemed socialized living; she was aware that Ranger Fox would like a curfew, a control over night-wandering souls such as she. Yet neither he nor her future tentmates could violate her independence or enjoyment of the surroundings. Others had disapproved of her ways at camp, but she had learned reticence and seldom clashed with anyone.

So here, she determined, Ranger Fox would not bully her if she kept a respectful distance. He meant well. She shuddered, remembering his suffocating kindness, his wanting to contain her life in social, accepted ways.

A last look at the remote and invulnerable stars reassured her as she walked back to the tent.

Long before the sun climbed over the cliffs, Molly was up and dressed in jeans and sweat shirt.

After a quick breakfast, she explored outside for a bed site. Azalea bushes were in bloom, and a few dogwood trees showed delicate white blossoms. Hulking granite boulders shouldered above them both. She found a spot near the tent, yet sheltered from view by boulders and thick cedar trees. There she placed a cot, mattress, and sleeping bag, covering them neatly with a waterproof tarp. Then she hefted her small footlocker beside it for table, cupboard, and closet. Well-pleased, she looked at the view she would have at night.

She whirled as she heard a tentative "Hi" and saw her stone-skipping friend climbing over a boulder. "Neat," he praised her camp. A grin shoved his freckles every which way. "Dad won't like it, but he won't find out from me."

She hesitated, not wanting the boy to have the idea she was defying his father. "Snake bite to a sleeping person is about as likely as being struck by lightning."

"What about bears?" he asked, eyes wide. "They raided the garbage cans most every night last summer."

She grinned. "I won't keep food anywhere near my bed, and I'll keep a flashlight and rocks handy to frighten them. Say, Foxy, want to give me a hand putting my bicycle together?"

While they were working in the shady parking area, a young man in a green ranger's uniform stopped. "Ah, a girl after my own heart," he hailed cheerfully. "I brought my bike too; it's the best way to escape traffic."

Molly glanced up shyly at a face that matched the voice—cheerful and friendly, with blue eyes under a mop of sandy hair. "Good exercise, too," she answered.

"Since Foxy won't introduce me," the young man made a mocking bow, "I will. Ranger-naturalist Tim McCorkle, a bike rider from way back, at your service."

No answering banter popped into Molly's mind, but Foxy rescued her, saying breezily, "This is Ranger-naturalist Molly Bishop, Camp 19's new ranger in skirts."

Molly managed, "You mean, ranger in grease."

Just then Breck Fox clobbered the companionship with a hearty, "Good morning, good morning. Shall we all ride over to the museum in my car?"

"No, thanks. I'm riding my bike." Tim left hastily.

"Brewster, your mother wants you. I see you're riding too, my dear. I would suggest some soap and water to remove the grease before you present yourself at the museum. Don't be late."

Seething, Molly watched him stride off. Was he going to harass her indefinitely because of her independence? Must he sound like an admonishing father? She hurried back to the tent, washed, changed into a dress, yanked a comb through her hair, and applied lipstick. The mirrored image of neatness reassured her, though she wished she had set her hair the night before.

17

CHAPTER II

Molly parked her bike in front of the vine-hugged museum, and looked beyond it to the white, thundering cataract of Yosemite Falls plunging down from a cliff top 2,400 feet above. The falls reminded her that Yosemite was a living museum of awesome features. She lowered her eyes and met the smiling gaze of a young, khaki-clad man.

Reluctantly, she followed a group of rangers inside the cool museum, up the stairs, and into a low-ceilinged room crowded with men and desks. Dissonant words reverberated, making her long to retreat to the open air and pinpointed noise of the falls.

Breck Fox caught her eye; he patted an empty chair and mouthed, "I saved it for you."

"Thanks, but I'd rather sit in back." Against the wall, Tim McCorkle and the khaki-clad man shared a table perch with her.

Noise dwindled to quiet as Chief Naturalist Hudson

entered and stood before the large stone fireplace hearth. "Welcome to Yosemite National Park. During the next five-day training period you will have an opportunity to become acquainted with every Park operation from research to maintenance, concessions to campfire talks, law enforcement to group singing, wildlife to firefighting. You will hear various experts outline their jobs and realize your responsibilities to Park visitors as an employee of the National Park Service."

He paused, fingering the arrowhead-shaped NPS insignia on his sleeve; then continued, smiling. "I'm proud to be a naturalist and of my career in helping visitors appreciate their Park. Yosemite contains 1,200 square miles, 700 miles of trails, three groves of *Sequoia giganteas,* living glaciers, waterfalls, meadows, and granite domes. It is a place of national significance and unique beauty. In this busy week, you will be cramming facts about the preservation, protection, and interpretation of Yosemite into your heads. Much of this orientation will be passed on to visitors. Now I want to introduce the Park Superintendent, who will outline the human organization necessary in operating Yosemite."

Molly listened, made notes, and felt a tingle of pride that she was to be a part of the dedicated, green-uniformed men who spoke so earnestly and humanely on different jobs. By five o'clock she had writer's cramp and tired ears from listening to numerous speakers. There was to be a two-and-a-half-hour break before the evening session on fire control, and she shot out the door of the training room as the last speaker said, "Dismissed."

She skipped stairs in her hurry to escape, grabbed

her bicycle, and vaulted on. Another fleeing figure passed her, the blond, khaki-clad man she had heard called Dutch. He was tall and lean with a look of hardness to him from his taut muscles to his contoured, glacial face. His eyes were the flinty blue of high Sierra lakes. Only his hair, crisp, straw-blond, seemed lively and uncontrolled. It spilled over his wrinkled forehead.

He hesitated. "Running away?"

She nodded, shuddering. "Too many people, too much talk, and too much confinement."

He smiled, eyes suddenly sparkling. "John Muir advised, 'Climb the mountains and get their good tidings. Nature's peace will flow into you as sunshine flows into trees. The winds will blow their own freshness into you, and the storms their energy, while cares will drop off like autumn leaves.' "

"Thank you," she said feelingly, "I'll take that advice." She pedaled rapidly to Happy Isles, where the turbulent river drowned out the conversations of knots of people. Placing her bicycle in a rack, she walked swiftly across the bridge and onto the asphalt trail to Vernal Fall. Many people trooped down towards camps, hotels, dinners; few walked upward as she did, head high, shoulders back, and senses alive. Every wild flower caused an observant stop; birds meant detours, and often she cut off the trail to examine a bush, tree, or rock. Careful notes were added to a nature notebook carried in her shoulder-hung purse. Memory stored bird calls, the plunging noise of the river, and, at length, the grand tumult of Vernal Fall. Near its foot, she flung herself down on sun-warmed boulders and gazed entranced.

Muir's words came true. "Nature's peace will flow into you as sunshine flows into trees." Contentedly, she thought of John Muir—naturalist, conservationist, mountaineer—one of the pioneers who had explored Yosemite on foot and in written word for others in the late 1800's.

Though Galen Clark, James Hutchings, and other pioneers had helped, more than any other person Muir had been responsible for shaping public and political feeling into the creation of Yosemite as a National Park.

Long shadows warned her of sunset and the evening session. A footrace and bicycle dash invigorated her soul and stimulated her appetite. At Camp 19, she had time only to changes clothes before arriving, breathless, at the Rangers' Clubhouse for the fire control discussion. Her stomach growled from her chocolate-bar dinner.

The second morning of training was equally as confining and information-filled about National Park history, philosophy, and services. Beginning with the afternoon session the training would be aimed directly at seasonal ranger-naturalists. The seasonal protective rangers, having absorbed principles, policies, legal and preservation matters, left to man patrol cars, entrance stations, trail crews, outposts, and other protective jobs.

At one o'clock, Ranger Hudson faced the thinned rank of twenty-two Ranger-naturalists with a comradely "Let's Get Acquainted" talk during which they were all introduced and backgrounds outlined.

"Molly Bishop is the only woman here so far," Dale Hudson added, after introducing her, "but two others are due here momentarily. Gloria Denning, a seasonal ranger-naturalist, will be returning for her third summer, and Laura Hamilton, our museum curator, for her second season.

"Molly is new to Yosemite, but old and wise to woods, sciences, and crafts. Glad to have you with us, Molly."

"Thanks," she mumbled, embarrassed, yet pleased to be pinpointed by speech and stared at by the curious men. At coffee and lunch breaks, they gathered together; but she, tired of people and confinement indoors, dashed outside for sun and air and freedom. Consequently, while the new men became acquainted, she grew familiar only with such things as the wild flower garden, the simulated Indian Village, and the pioneer cemetery.

In her scant evening time at Camp 19, she explored the talus slope back of the tents and observed wildlife tracks. There she met many of the camp children, led by Foxy, who questioned her, followed her, and aimlessly formed a nature study group.

Breck Fox insisted on driving her to the third morning's training session. He complained, "I've been trying to have a word with you, my dear, about joining in camp activities. You have yet to stop for a visit at any of the tents or come to a gabfest after evening session. Don't be shy; join us. How about tonight? Betty's making cookies."

"I'm busy tonight," she answered defensively. "Sorry." His fatherliness, his almost commanding invitations, frightened her. It was impossible to explain her need for aloneness. Her busyness that night would be with flashlight and notebook, observing wildlife from her outdoor bed.

"You are a lone wolf, aren't you?" Breck parked the car. "You might like us if you gave us a chance."

Feeling alien and misunderstood, she slid from the car. She knew he deserved an explanation and wanted an apology, but shyness, and the vast gulf between their personalities, blocked clearing words. "Thanks for the ride," she managed, and hurried toward the museum.

Instead of going upstairs, she ducked outside to the wild flower garden, her thoughts in turmoil. She had been rude, but he had inspired it. If only he would leave her alone! In time she would acquaint herself with the camp adults; it was enough now that she was with people all day. She stared at a blooming mariposa lily, envying its peace and self-reliance.

Dutch touched her shoulder. "Pretty, isn't it? Proud, alone. Muir wrote, 'Earth has no sorrows that earth cannot heal. . . .' "

Did he understand? Did people *en masse* overwhelm him too? She looked at his brown, abstracted face; its features were strong and angular, stamped with independence; his wheatblond hair was long and wild. His name, besides "Dutch," was Amos Vanderbunt. Ranger Hudson had introduced him as a botany professor from a small men's college. Were they alike? She met his deep blue eyes for a moment and was warmed.

Then, impersonally, matter-of-factly, he said, "Come on or we'll be late."

Molly found that morning session engrossing. Though there was not a complete lecture on Junior Rangers, there many references to the program, particularly group singing, conducting nature walks.

At the lunch break she stopped by the post office for mail, and was given a bulky package. Her uniform! She shot for Camp 19 on her bike.

Chatter halted her before she entered the tent. Two cheerful women's voices trilled. Molly's spirits drooped. Her treasured solitude was ended. Reluctantly she entered and saw that the tent was hung, draped, and piled with billowy dresses, skirts, and sweaters. Perfume scented the air and high heels graced the wood stove.

A trim, golden-haired girl emerged from the back tent. Her smile showed perfect teeth, dimples, and sparkling blue eyes. "You must be Molly! Hello. I'm Gloria Denning, the other Ranger-naturalist. Laura, come meet our tentmate."

While Gloria chattered on, apologizing for her mess, Molly stared in disbelief. How could this utterly feminine fashion plate of a girl be a naturalist with a knowledge of animals, bugs, and plant life?

A large, rawboned, gray-haired woman came in to shake Molly's hand. Gloria introduced her. "Laura Hamilton, our museum curator."

Laura's voice was surprisingly motherly. "My dear, I'm glad to meet you. Will you join us in a cup of tea?"

"Yes, thank you." Molly felt she needed something bracing after the shock of meeting her dissimilar, overpowering tentmates. The hot tea made on the camp stove was good, but the barrage of questions and chitchat about Camp 19 left her drained and defenseless.

Gloria released her from social torment. "Your uniform came; I can tell from the box beside you. Aren't you dying to try it on?"

"Yes. Excuse me." Molly found the back tent a clutter of women's apparel, suitcases, and half-unpacked boxes. Quickly she undid her package. The uniform skirt was plain, straight, and olive green like the men's trousers. There was a pleat in the back, loops for a self-fabric belt, and a slash pocket in front. She approved the skirt's plainness and the matching long-sleeved, three-button jacket. It was given authority by the arrowhead emblem of the National Park Service sewn on the left shoulder, and the USNPS silver letters pinned on the collar. Similarly the air-hostess-type hat was made official by the arrowhead-shaped NPS insignia showing a picturesque sequoia tree against snowcapped mountains. That insignia meant belonging to the NPS, being an official representative not just of Yosemite, but of many National Parks and National Monuments in the United States.

With a thrill of pride, she set the hat on her head. She was a Park Service employee—a Ranger-naturalist.

A white, short-sleeved blouse, hose, brown high-heeled shoes, and gloves she had brought with her completed the uniform which she donned hurriedly. She surveyed herself in a small mirror. Except for her hair, which needed combing, she appeared neat, trim, official!

Shyly, she walked into the front tent. "Charming, my dear," Laura applauded vocally.

Lips pursed, blue eyes narrowed, Gloria scrutinized Molly. Finally, she said, "Your skirt's miles too long. I'll hem it."

"Thanks." Molly glanced at her wristwatch. "Not now though. I'm due back at the training room."

"So am I," Gloria answered carelessly. "You can bike over there in three minutes. Now, hop up on that bench."

"It's all right. I don't care," Molly protested.

"Maybe you don't, but I do. There aren't many women rangers in the Service, and we're proud of our appearance as well as our performance. Laura, will you pin the hem while I fold it up?"

Efficiency and command replaced femininity in Gloria. Cowed, Molly stood quietly, her unruly stomach growling audibly, disconcertingly.

"Good heavens," Gloria chuckled, "you haven't eaten, have you?"

Molly mumbled, "I haven't had time."

"Here, you can have half my sandwich." Gloria went after a hearty, man-sized meat and cheese sandwich which Molly took without argument. Gloria was a mystery; pretty and charming, yet efficient and bossy; petite, yet possessed of a big appetite.

"There." Gloria stood, looking once again at the skirt. "The pins will hold it to the dinner break, and then I'll hem it. Now comb your hair, add some lipstick, and you'll do the Park Service proud."

Molly had no time for surprise at Gloria's bike riding or tomboyishness in her headlong hurry to race the girl and the clock. Seconds ahead of her challenger, she raced into the museum. Ranger Fox spoke coldly from behind the information desk. "You're three minutes late, Ranger Bishop."

All Molly heard as she tore upstairs was the transforming word "Ranger." Nothing else—her lateness, his reprimand—mattered.

When she arrived back at camp, Laura had dinner ready. "It would be nice to have dinner together often." Laura served the suggestion along with creamed tuna. "We could take turns cooking."

Molly recoiled at the idea of tying herself down to social meals. "I couldn't," she blurted. "I'm busy evenings."

"Of course." Laura's mouth drooped. "Dates and campfire talks. I understand. My hours are from eight to five. Sometimes the evenings alone are long." Her squarish face was sad, her gray eyes bleak with lonesomeness. To Molly, she looked like a storied old maid—kindly, left out, and prudish. She dismissed the statement by explaining that her evening busyness wasn't dates but hiking, exploring, and observing nature.

After the evening session was over, Molly saw Gloria drive off with Tim McCorkle and Dutch Vanderbunt. Wryly, she wondered if he had an apt Muir quote for Gloria.

Molly's own need for "nature's peace" made her hurry by the noisy camps. Campfire smoke stung her eyes and her face felt stiff and lifeless. Somehow, she had survived the demandingly long, social day and wanted only rest and privacy. Always before, solitude had been an anticipated pleasure; now, besides that, it was a retreat, an escape medium she needed to survive the people-thronged days.

Talk spouted from the Fox's tent, reminding her of Breck's invitation. Light shone from her tent which, seemingly, was broadcasting a baseball game. Laura must be a fan. Molly couldn't face entering the tent for pajamas, scores, and more sociability. Instead she retreated to her hidden, peaceful cot, where sleep came.

Robins, warbling happiness, awoke her. After a hurried shower in the washhouse she walked back to the tent wide awake and hungry.

As Molly began fixing breakfast, Laura appeared in the doorway of the sleeping tent. Her gray hair was in curlers, her eyes held anger, her words were glacial.

"Good morning. It's a relief to have you home again *at last!*"

Gloria crowded in, less sarcastically. "Really, Molly, even the best beach parties break up before dawn! Couldn't you have staggered home a little earlier?"

Laura sniffed, "Of course, there's no curfew or regulations about times girls should be in camp at night, but even Gloria was home by one-thirty. I couldn't help worrying about you."

Molly whooped with laughter at their mistake. "I was in bed by ten."

"Really!" Laura's tone climbed in volume and outrage. "And just where did you sleep? Not in this tent, I know. Perhaps, in a tree?"

"No, under a tree." Laughter kept bubbling into her voice at the thought of their wild misapprehensions about her. "Sleeping outside has been part of summer to me since I was in pigtails, so I found a perfect spot for my bed in a rocky alcove out back. I'm sorry you didn't know. I didn't mean to worry anyone."

Gloria recovered her poise with a laugh. "Breck told me you were a lone wolf; this proves it. Is that coffee water boiling? May I have some? Thanks."

Laura's righteousness merged into shocked concern. "My dear, out there by yourself, surrounded by darkness and animals! Aren't you afraid of bears?"

Gloria saved her from making futile explanations by saying, "Don't forget to pack a lunch. This is your last day of training, tour day, when you sight-see and watch other naturalists perform."

"Are you going?"

"Yes. I have had the training; but Dutch and I, as old-timers, will go along with some of the permanent men as guides and chauffeurs. There will be several cars going. We gals will stick together in Dutch's station wagon."

"Does he qualify as an old-timer?"

"I should say so! This is his seventh summer."

Molly was curious. "He doesn't look more than twenty-one."

"He's twenty-four; but he worked here while he was still in college. He's a nut about Yosemite botany, history, conservation. . . ."

"John Muir," Molly suggested.

"Isn't he though? This summer he's researching for a book on Muir as a mountaineer. Hurry up with that lunch. I don't want to keep him waiting."

Everything about the day delighted Molly. The air was crisp and fragrant with mingled odors of pine, azalea, and bear clover. Their first stop was at the Mariposa Grove of giant sequoias where they heard another lecture; but this one, held right among the trees, was thoroughly enjoyable. She stood back from the crowd, every sense alert, awed by the enormous, century-spanning trees.

"Just think," she remarked quietly to Dutch, "some of these trees are five thousand years old! I wonder what Muir would have said about them."

Hands shoved in his pockets, fair head thrust back, eyes gazing up, he recited slowly, "And here are visions too, and dreams, and a splendid set of ghosts, too many for ink and narrow paper."

"Thank you," she said, touched, feeling an odd excitement that, at last, she had found a man she could communicate with on her own level.

Next the caravan stopped at Wawona where there were stables, campgrounds, a charming old hotel, and other recreational facilities.

Dale Hudson explained, "Wawona—an Indian word for big trees—was the first area of the Park to be explored and developed back in 1856. Recently, the Park Service has moved historic buildings to Wawona to make a Pioneer History Center. As we tour it, you will notice that the covered bridge, one of the few left in the West, links the exhibits of pioneer housing and modes of transportation."

After a Ranger-naturalist lectured on the stories of each historic building, Molly examined the restoration and the furnishings with pleasure. Several times she entered into conversations with other trainees. She knew them casually from camp and training sessions, but discovered them at the Pioneer Center as individuals. Instead of sitting apart at lunch time, she was drawn into the group, and Molly surprised herself by being interested in, and contributing to, discussions. Their talk was mostly about the Park, preservation, and wildlife.

Irving Dawson, whom she had known only as a father of four camp youngsters, asked her about the low-growing, witch-hazel-smelling bush growing around them.

"That's bear clover, *Chamaebatia foliolosa*, sometimes known as *kit-kit-dizze*, but usually called mountain misery."

"But why?" Irving asked. "It makes a lawnlike carpet under the pines, and that white bloom has a pungent smell."

"Pungent is right!" Molly grinned. "Try hiking through it, and your jeans and boots will be pungent for weeks."

Further talk established Irving to be from Iowa. "There we have hardwood trees. Stop by the tent tonight, and I'll show you some pictures of Iowa mammals and birds," he invited.

For the first time she felt at ease and self-confident with the men, even wondered if she should not join the camp get-togethers sometimes.

Although she had visited Glacier Point with her parents and had read extensively on the geology of Yosemite, Molly found new fascination in looking 3,214 feet down to the floor of Yosemite Valley. Everything appeared in miniature. The museum, post office, and stores were toy buildings; minute, colored dots on the meandering river were air mattresses. Mirror Lake seemed an insignificant pond, and the Camp Curry swimming pool looked like nothing more than a square-cut turquoise.

"Absorbing, isn't it?" Tim joined her. "Too bad the cliff hides Camp 19, but look at Camp 7 with its tiny tents and bug-like cars."

31

"No wonder the firefall's so spectacular," Molly said, looking around at the pile of red fir bark that would be burned later, then pushed over the cliff in a fiery cascade of coals, to be watched by awed Yosemite Valley visitors.

Tim shrugged. "A man-made wonder. I prefer Nature's feats. Come on, let's go listen to the geology talk."

After that was over, Molly backed away from the visitors who streamed by clutching children, ice cream bars, and cameras. "Too many people," she complained to Gloria.

"Yosemite is for people, remember?" Gloria said seriously. "They are part owners too, just as you and I are."

"Nevertheless, I'm glad my assignment is Junior Rangers where I'll be with children, not adults."

Dutch regarded her quizzically. "Adults are just children grown-up with capacities for wonder and admiration, too."

"I can't talk to them," she confessed. "Maybe I'm still a child at heart."

Windburned and carefree, she enjoyed the stop at the half-empty Bridalveil Campground.

"Why aren't people camped here where there's space and coolness instead of jammed, tent to tent, in Yosemite Valley?"

Irving enthused, "This place has conveniences too: washhouses, piped water, tables. . . . I can't understand why more visitors aren't here."

Eyebrows lifted, Dutch spoke quietly. "Maybe this story will help explain. Last summer a visitor asked me where he could camp away from the mob. I directed him to Tamarack Flat, a wonderful little camp, three miles off the beaten highway. The man said, 'Fine. Thanks a lot, Ranger. Say, is there a movie near there?' "

Molly was indignant. "That's the trouble with people; they want conveniences and civilization in the wilderness."

"Don't be too harsh, Molly," Irving advised. "Many of those ignorant-seeming visitors are from Pennsylvania and New Jersey or other highly urban, civilized states. Wilderness awes and frightens them. They need to be near other people, stores, and, yes, even noise for reassurance against the wildness and surrounding grandeur. Be patient with them. As naturalists we can help them better understand, appreciate, and use their Park."

"Well said." Dutch clapped a hand across Irving's shoulders. "You'll make a good naturalist."

Irving's face colored. "Thanks. Coming from you, that's a real compliment."

For a moment Molly felt letdown, and judged as intolerant.

At five the caravan arrived back at the museum where Ranger Hudson addressed them. "I won't keep you cooped up long," he promised; then he explained that the Junior Ranger program wouldn't begin until July first, "when funds are available. Meanwhile, there will be preparation, campfire talks, and duty stations."

Molly recoiled. A week before Junior Rangers! An

endless time, jam-packed with the kind of public things she dreaded.

The ranger continued, "The information desk must be attended, and two geology talks and two Indian talks must be given daily out back in the Indian Village. After observing and listening a few times, you new trainees will take over these talks.

"Remember, at all times, your job is that of interpreting Yosemite to visitors by answering and raising questions, by making the Park meaningful to them. Remember, too, like you, every Park visitor is part owner of Yosemite National Park, and is entitled to respect and courtesy from you no matter how foolish his questions may sound. Good luck."

Each trainee was handed a work schedule sheet as he filed out. Before studying it, Molly carried hers into the wildflower garden. Quickly, she scanned the print. Number 7 was Bishop; she was assigned to 23, 9 and 18 stations. According to the code, 23 was the information desk, 9 the Indian talk, 18 the geology talk.

Fright seized her. All three duty stations involved people descending on helpless her. Of course, she wouldn't have to give talks for a while, just observe; but she would have to answer questions, and sell Park literature at the desk.

The granite cliffs seemed to imprison her in the Valley. She had heard Tim describe manning the information desk as "lizard duty." "It's like sitting on your tail in the sun, blinking your eyes and answering questions."

Yes, she thought frantically, but a lizard could slither off; she would be trapped behind the desk.

CHAPTER III

1437194

She plodded heavily across asphalt paths toward camp, depressed and stormy. Shrieking jays made her look across to a lush meadow where a deer was eating from a small girl's hand. A boy of about six was stroking the doe's back. "Look, Mama, she likes being patted!"

Camera-aiming "Mama" and her equally occupied husband were busy taking pictures and directing. "Move back a little, Son. That's right. Now, Ginny, hold that cookie away from the deer's mouth so she'll have to stretch her head for it. Perfect!"

However, the doe spoiled the picture by reaching up one dainty hoof and striking at the cookie-tempting girl. Anticipating this, Molly ran and pulled the child back as the doe bounded off.

"You ruined the shot!" the man exclaimed angrily.

The girl cried, "That deer hitted me."

Her brother agreed. "If the ranger hadn't grabbed Sissy, her face would have been cut. Wow!"

"Wow is right," Molly commented, trying to calm her own fright and anger before explaining. "Though they appear tame, deer are wild animals. When people withdraw food from them, they're likely to strike with their sharp hooves and rake a face or a shoulder."

"Why, that could scar her for life!" the father fumed. "deer are dangerous!"

"Yes," Molly agreed, "they are when their natural habits are interrupted. There's a law against feeding or molesting deer or bear. What you feed them may harm them, and what they might do would harm you."

"Goodness," the mother said, drawing the girl to her side. "We just arrived here, and we didn't know."

"We'll never feed or pet another deer." Sober nods from the children backed up their father's heartfelt statement. "Thank you, Ranger."

Molly walked off, satisfied that she had warned four visitors, without angering them, on one of the real but little-understood, dangers of the Park.

When Gloria and Laura set off that evening to observe a campfire talk, Molly stayed behind to study the Information Handbook, and map of Yosemite. She was still at it when Laura came home. Arriving from a date, Gloria breezed in. "What are you doing?"

"Cramming my head with facts, elevations, and names so I can answer questions on desk duty tomorrow."

Gloria reached over, closed her book, and turned off the lamp. "Go to bed," she ordered cordially. "The two most popular questions asked by visitors are 'Where are the rest rooms,' and 'When does the firefall fall?' "

Molly seated herself behind the information

desk a full five minutes before eight A.M. Glass cases on two sides of her displayed the many park publications for sale. Maps hung on racks above her, and a small closet to her right contained extra copies. "As a last resort," she remembered Dale Hudson lecturing "call one of us old hands upstairs when you can't answer a question." An SOS squawk box hung in the closet above the telephone.

She polished the counter, rearranged some booklets, checked change in the cash register, cleared her throat, and looked out the open doors to the sunlit world. A buzzy fly entered the museum, but no visitors. A couple of late arriving rangers hailed her and pounded up the stairs, but she remained alone with the desk.

At eight-twenty, concluding that all visitors slept late on Saturday, she began reading a trail guide.

"Hey, lady, is he alive?"

A small, solemn voice pulled her out of the booklet. A round-eyed boy in short pants stood by the door, regarding her soberly.

"What?"

Patiently pointing toward the mounted owl in the glass case, he boy repeated, "Is he alive?"

"No."

"Are you sure?"

His seriousness amused her. "Yes, I'm sure."

"Then why is he staring at me?"

Carefully, concealing laughter, she explained that owl's eyes always seemed to look starey and wise. After seeing pictures in the bird booklet, he was reassured. Then his parents questioned her as to what easy hike they could take their boy on where he might see wildlife.

She suggested a walk through the meadows, thinking that if all questions were that easy and from such friendly people, desk duty would be easy.

After that people began to knot in front of the desk, asking mostly routine questions. Where's Mirror Lake? Are there any bear in the Valley? How high is Half Dome? What bird makes the honking sound? Where's a good place to fish? We have this afternoon to see the park; where shall we go?

Once she heard a triumphant cry, "Look, I'm a glacier!" and looked over, horrified, to see a small boy lying on the relief model of Yosemite Park. Twice she had to remove the map's pointer stick from youngsters using it as a spear. Another time a small, tow-headed boy elbowed his way through the crowd to the counter and asked engagingly, "Hey, do you guys have any bathrooms around here?"

She concluded that the job wasn't dull, but felt trapped by people. Her stomach knotted, but her voice remained calm and courteous until Irving relieved her a little before ten-thirty.

Dale Hudson caught up with her as she walked toward the Indian Village. "Tired?"

"So many people," she shuddered, "so many questions. It's unnerving. I'm not built for public appearances. Will I have to give talks here?"

"Eventually," he nodded. "You needn't worry about the Indian talk; at USC that day I found your knowledge of Indian life most thorough."

"Thanks. I am familiar with the tribes that frequented the San Bernardino mountains, mostly because an old chief, who lived near camp, taught me history, ceremony, and some practical things like making arrowheads." Molly frowned doubtfully. "But the life and customs of the Yosemite Ahwahneeches were different and I won't know what to say."

"Sure you will. Don't let visitors scare you. Remember, they come to talks because they are eager to learn some of the history of Yosemite. Just listen to me sound off this morning, and you'll see how simple it is to speak."

Molly noted several other trainees in the audience who sat on logs facing an Indian sweat house and two cedar-bark, teepee-like structures called *umachas*.

Dale spoke with a relaxed but competent air, outlining tribal life in the Valley, how it was interrupted by white men who came nearby in the California gold rush, and what fine basket weavers the Ahwahneeches had been.

Children and adults listened attentively as he talked. "They were children of nature and most of their food supply was from nature and procured by bow and arrow or pickings. Can you tell us some of the things they ate and how they prepared them, Ranger Bishop?"

There was no time for astonishment or fright with the audience waiting, and the answers in her mind. Molly stood, gulped once, riveted her gaze on a group of youngsters, and spoke clearly. "Mortar holes like these in the pockmarked rock were made by Indian women grinding acorns into a meal. Like bread to us, acorns were a chief staple of diet for the Ahwahneeches. They had them for breakfast, lunch, and dinner in a mush, thin soup, or patties which they baked on hot, flat rocks. One summer I experimented with acorns, grinding, leaching, cooking, and taking some bites of meal." She paused, smiling. "Evidently my taste buds were lacking; I didn't want seconds."

Twice more during his talk, Ranger Hudson turned to her for factual comments. Because she knew the subject, and it was a spontaneous referral, Molly found it easy to talk.

Afterwards Dale teased her gently. "See, people don't bite. Your facts and firsthand experience impressed them."

"Thanks, but I won't always have you to run interference."

"You won't need me. Just have faith in yourself. I do."

A freckled child questioned, "Say, Ranger, how didja make that acorn stuff?"

After she had satisfied the girl, adult lingerers had pertinent questions. When Molly was through answering them, she looked around for the big ranger. He was gone and she knew, gladly, that she hadn't needed him. Inwardly she thanked him for his shepherding of her into a public talk. It, the listeners' obvious interest, and the title "Ranger" addressed to her gave her a heady feeling of success.

During her afternoon stint on desk duty, there was no time for worry, reading, or boredom. She kept busy selling pamphlets, answering questions, and politely asking youngsters to finish their ice cream or candy outdoors. A park regulation required visitors to be properly dressed in order to enter the museum. Embarrassed but firm, she had to ask several teen-agers in bathing suits to leave.

Directly after Breck gave the afternoon geology talk, people flocked to the desk to buy geology and Indian pamphlets. The other day-long best seller was the *Self-Guiding Auto Tour of Yosemite.*

Twice she had to use the squawk box to call a ranger to answer an involved question; once on Park policy regarding roads, once on the history of cattle-raising adjacent to the boundaries.

Most of the questioners were courteous, but a few were antagonistic. "Can you tell me *why* we weren't warned at the entrance station that the hotel was full?" "Just because I picked a few little dogwood blossoms, a ranger had fits." "I can't find the Indian caves. Why don't you put up more road signs?" "Why can't you do something about the mosquitoes?"

At times Molly felt besieged by questions. Then some visitor would thank her for identifying a bird from a verbal description or say, "I certainly enjoyed the geology talk. You rangers are doing a wonderful job explaining nature," and she would be proud that she was part of the Park Service.

Five o'clock quitting time loomed in her mind as release, and freedom. Her relief was ten minutes late.

Finally, Breck Fox pushed in the swinging gate. "Guess I'm a little tardy. Sorry."

Her anger was interrupted by a gum-chewing teenager. "What time is it, Doll?"

She stared at the big wall clock behind the boy's head, enunciating sarcastically, "Five-eleven and a half."

The boy turned away and Breck asked icily, "Did you need to be rude?"

Face flaming, she exploded, "I'm tired of stupid questions like 'Does that road have to be so curvy?' Haven't people ever seen a mountain road before?"

Breck answered sharply, "No. Many visitors have never seen mountains before. If you came from flatland Kansas, for instance, you might be scared and full of questions too." In a less formidable tone, he began, "A ranger-naturalist needs to be. . . ."

Molly grabbed her purse and rushed out, partly to escape the deserved lecture and partly to miss questions from a gang of Girl Scouts converging on the desk. Outside she mounted her bike and pedaled for the comparative peace of Camp 19. Breck's rebuke, her rudeness, the tiring public day reeled hornet-like in her mind. A rescuing thought steered her into camp—her two days off had begun officially at five. She was free for the next forty-eight hours; free to go, to seek perspective, peace.

Both Gloria and Laura were in the tent cooking dinner. Their idle talk irritated Molly. Aloneness was impossible here. Impulsively, she hurried to her bed, rolled up her sleeping bag, found her back pack, and loaded them into her dusty, unused car.

Next she braved the tent for food, a change of clothes, and a quickly packed suitcase. Questions pelted her as she packed foodstuff in a box. "Where are you going? Camping? Don't you want a lantern?"

"Camping," she answered; then realizing that their questions were kindly, added, "I need to be by myself and I want to see Yosemite's high country."

"Alone!" Laura wailed. "You're so young."

Stung, Molly said, "I'll be twenty next month."

Laura sighed. "I guess I'm an old worrywart; but if you go, you'll miss the camp potluck tomorrow. It's an annual affair; most of the outpost naturalists come in for it. You don't want to miss that!"

"Sorry, but I couldn't care less," Molly commented bluntly. Laura looked hurt, insulted.

Gloria interceded smoothly, "Molly just isn't social, Laura. Let her alone. The time away will do her good." She followed Molly out to the car.

"I'm sorry," muttered the younger girl. "I'm just not used to living so socially, and answering to others."

"I'm not condemning you, but, Molly, you need to be less immature and sensitive."

Molly flared, "What do you mean, immature? I'm independent."

"I should say so! But independence does not denote maturity. If you are questioned or advised, you misunderstand and fly to the woods. You act defensive."

Fists clenched and mind set, Molly demanded, "What's wrong with that? The woods give me the strength to face people."

Gloria sighed. "Think about it and remember life is spent mostly in company with people, not trees." Her blue eyes were troubled as she looked at Molly.

"If you want to be by yourself, try Tamarack Flat."

"Thanks." Molly drove off, emotions in a turmoil. Defensive? Immature? Could Gloria be right?

After miles of delightful mountain driving, she nosed her roadster onto a narrow, asphalt road where a sign read "Tamarack Flat—3 miles." The road was twisty, wild, and boulder-strewn, but she relaxed as she met no other cars. At the campground itself smoke pinpointed other campers stationed along a clear stream. Rude stone fireplaces and pit toilets were the only conveniences.

Juncos and chipmunks were obvious wildlife, but Molly's trained eye saw deer, bear, and porcupine tracks in the sandy creekside. A lovely confusion of tamarack pines, standing and fallen, green-lichened rocks, blooming columbines, willow, and bitter cherry bushes made her decide to stay.

She chose a campsite far up the creek. Her "bedroom" consisted of a tarp, air mattress, and sleeping bag; her "kitchen" a grill and frying pan over a rock firesite.

Her timesaving, tentless camp would shock Laura, Molly thought, amused; yet Muir and Galen Clark, Yosemite's famous mountaineers, would have scorned air mattresses and grills. They had traveled light with only blanket rolls, oatmeal, tea, and raisins; not her hearty, space-taking ham and eggs.

What Muir quotation could Dutch have produced for this evening, she wondered, thinking that he, with his quietness, would make a good camping companion.

Before the sun was up, she was dressed, fed, and away on foot on the wooded trail to the top of El Capitan. Along the flower-bordered way she noted browsing deer, one root-grubbing bear, a fox, and two coveys of mountain quail. Flycatchers, Sierra grouse, and vocal flickers kept her company. When the forest thinned to manzanita and some sentinel pines, she shed her jacket and drank from her canteen, feeling, contentedly, that her mind was stretching along with too-little-used muscles.

According to her topographical map, she was near

the Valley rim; but an hour elapsed before she reached it. Her many stops were for pleasure, observation, note-taking, and making flower sketches.

Before she trod the granite top of El Capitan, she had glimpses of grand views, realized fully from its highest point 7,584 feet above sea level. Slowly she sank down on a rock, overcome by the view of the Yosemite Valley and High Sierra peaks.

Perhaps, she thought, the views from Glacier Point were more breathtaking, but they had been reached by car and shared, sightwise and audibly, by many other people. Here she felt triumphant, a trail-follower, not a trail-maker, true; but a pioneer, proud as a conqueror.

After lunch she looked at the register attached to the snag and saw that she was only the second person to climb El Capitan dome that year. Amos Vanderbunt's name was scrawled boldly with a Memorial Day date and, predictably, a Muir quote: "El Capitan—Nature's steadfastness and power. . . ."

As she retraced her steps toward Ribbon Creek, she saw ant-speck cars scurrying out of the distant Wawona Tunnel; saw them and thought how a few days, two weeks at the most, would see them scurrying away, occupants' vacations over. Her own luck at staying the summer struck home. She resolved that no questioners, no speech, no criticism would scare her away. People loomed insignificant beside the giants she was among. Even though they might seem suffocating at times, she had two days a week to escape and explore every blessed peak.

Monday, she drove to Tioga Pass, toured Tuolumne Meadows with its patches of winter's snow, swam in chilly

Teneya Lake. She took no long hikes, but stopped often for exploratory walks to see snowplants, a tree riddled with woodpecker holes, a view. . . .

Below Crane Flat on the way back to camp, she pulled out at the scenic overlook of Big Meadow. A knot of excited people by a trash can reminded her forcibly of civilization. An excited boy called, "Hey, look, my dad killed a rattler!"

Molly walked toward the group, carefully framing a statement. "A National Park protects all wildlife, including ·snakes."

With smug triumph a burly man announced, "This is, or was, a rattlesnake. It was sneaking along in the weeds here by the garbage can when I nailed it with a rock. Rattlers are dangerous."

"Good thing Dad killed it before it bit someone," the boy stated proudly.

"Let me see, please." She had to crowd in to see the still-writhing brown gopher snake. "Good grief," she said violently, "that's not a rattlesnake; that's a harmless, mouse-eating gopher snake!"

Disconcerted, the man blustered, "How can you tell? What makes you a snake expert anyway?"

With effort she controlled her temper and voice so as to educate, not antagonize him. "There are no rattles on its tail," she pointed out, "and it has a narrow head with round pupils. A rattlesnake has a triangular-shaped head and slit eyes, with definite patterns on its skin. Notice this gopher snake has an irregular marking."

"Oh," the man was abashed. "Next time, I'll know. I'm from the city. You say a gopher snake eats mice?"

"Yes, it is one of the farmer's best friends."

"I thought all snakes were bad."

"Goodness, no." Animatedly, Molly gave an impromptu lecture on the differences between venomous and harmless snakes and of their benefit to mankind.

"You should be a ranger," the boy called after her.

"I am!" she chuckled as she climbed into the car.

"No kidding! Are you going to report us?"

"Not this time."

"There won't be a next time," the man shouted.

Molly drove on to camp, pleased that she had acted as a naturalist instead of a disgusted person. Her spontaneous lecture reassured her too. It had been easy, like talking to youngsters. She recalled that July first and Junior Rangers would cut short her week at desk duty.

Again the following morning she had her back to the wall answering questions, but her mountain-restored perspective kept her composed. Foxy was in and out with chatter and grave-faced questions. "Tell me, Madam, is there a volcano in the Park?"

Several information seekers lingered to talk interestedly of the Park and their visits to it. Responding, she asked counter questions, and told of her trip to the top of El Capitan.

Not only had she endured her two-hour stint of information duty, she thought, waiting for someone to relieve her, but she had enjoyed parts of it.

Gloria and Dale came down the stairs, both looking harassed. Molly cocked an eye at the clock.

Dale did too. "I know we're late for the Indian talk —Molly, will you give it, please?"

Her mouth fell open. "Now?—why I just couldn't."

"We're short-handed upstairs today, and two permanents have to escort some important visitors around. If you'll give the Indian talk and Gloria the geology one, I'll be off the hook."

"All right," she swallowed. "If you trust me, I guess I can."

"Good girl! Thanks," he beamed, and hurried out.

Molly shouldered her purse. "Wait," Gloria commanded. "Let me pretty you up."

Gloria straightened Molly's hat, tucked in her blouse, and handed her a rubber-tipped pointer stick. "For gesturing," she smiled, "and something to hang onto if you're nervous."

"*If?*" Molly echoed sickly. She started out, saw Foxy, and quavered, "Come with me?"

"Sure," he grinned reassuringly. "I wouldn't miss it; but hurry, people are waiting."

They ran up the path to the Indian circle where a crowd waited sitting on logs. Faces blurred before Molly's eyes as she stepped into the circle. Numbly, she opened her mouth to speak, but no words came as formed in her mind. Where was Foxy? Her eyes found him next to a familiar-looking boy who whispered audibly, "Hey, Dad, it's the snake ranger."

As people smiled at that, Molly relaxed enough to say spontaneously, "One good thing about Indian life was that it was unhurried. There were no deadlines, no clocks, nobody waiting. . . ." Smiling faces encouraged her. "I'm sorry to be late. I'm Ranger-naturalist Molly Bishop, and on behalf of the Department of Interior and

48

the National Park Service, I want to welcome you to Yosemite.

"Prior to 1851," her gaze was on Foxy, "the Ahwahneeche Indians lived in this Valley. Instead of houses with wall-to-wall carpeting, they lived in bark *umachas*, like this, with wall-to-wall dirt. Instead of electric blankets, they used animal skins for warmth."

Foxy was mouthing something. She deciphered it as "slow down," and did, daring to look at other faces. Even adult expressions seemed interested, friendly. The youngsters were as responsive as any she had ever addressed.

"Because there were no handy food markets, Indian braves hunted deer and caught fish. Even ants and the supposedly tasty ka-cha-vee fly were eaten for protein. Grasshoppers were roasted; clover was eaten raw. Acorn mush, gruel, and cakes were prepared by the Indian women, who didn't have a single labor-saving device in their outdoor kitchens. Instead of pills to aid digestion, California Bay nuts with clover were chewed.

"When the women weren't cooking, gathering food, or taking care of their children, they were weaving fine, intricate baskets like these by the rock. Each basket had a specific purpose. There were carrying baskets, cooking baskets, papoose carriers, and baskets so tightly woven they held water."

Molly talked on enthusiastically, and when she was finished, applause broke out. Many people stayed behind to ask questions which she answered confidently. When the last man walked away, saying, "Thanks, Ranger. I enjoyed your talk," she glowed inwardly.

CHAPTER IV

From behind the desk, Gloria teased, "Stop your glowing!"

"What?" Happiness bubbled up in Molly.

"Your face would have told me that your talk was a huge success even if fifty-four visitors hadn't charged in right after it to buy the Indian booklet. You certainly spurred interest, 'Big-Chieftess-Running-Off-at-the-Mouth,' despite your qualms."

Molly defended herself sheepishly. "Half the audience were children; so after the first horrible moments, it was like the talking I've done at summer camp."

Gloria unloaded baskets from Foxy's arms. "Here, I'll take these and you take this." She flipped him a quarter. "And go treat our far-from-tongue-tied friend to an ice cream cone."

"But. . . ." Molly started to protest and was stopped by the frown on Gloria's face. "We're going, we're going. And thanks."

As she and Foxy trod the thronged walk to an ice cream stand, Molly reflected that Gloria was bossy in a nice way. Several times she had brought home malts or ice cream, saying flippantly, "You and Laura are such beanpoles; it's my civic duty to fatten you up!"

Before Molly had gone to bed after her camping trip, Gloria had commented, "You look like a sheepdog. Let me set that mop you call hair."

Pretty, popular, and blunt-spoken Gloria had seemed an unlikely friend, but Molly knew, warmly, that she could be counted on.

Breck passed by just as Foxy handed her a chocolate double decker. He raised his eyebrows, consulted his watch, and said heavily, "Well, well, a little ice cream break, hey? Don't be gone too long from duty."

His remarks popped the balloon of excitement surrounding her. She felt derelict and defensive. While she sought for an answer that wouldn't sound surly, Foxy explained lightly, "Gloria's orders, Dad. Here, have a bite."

"Thanks. See you at campfire tonight, Molly."

After the big man walked off sucking ice cream, his son said, "You two always bristle at each other. Give him a chance; he's really a good guy."

"Of course," she agreed quickly, thinking that Breck made opportunities to give her a bad time. "What did he mean about campfire?"

"Oh, lots of nights after making talks, everybody jams into one tent or around a campfire. You know about that."

"Yes." She knew her avoidance of the gatherings

annoyed Breck. "Where's the campfire held tonight?"

"In the fire circle near your tent." Foxy gazed at her, worriedly. "You'll come?"

"Naturally," she answered, wondering sardonically if she had a choice.

"Look." Foxy's freckles twisted in a frown. "You're going to go to campground talks this week, aren't you?"

"Yes," she answered, "it's part of naturalist training to listen to the old-timers and see how it's done before preparing our own talks."

"Well, come with me tonight and listen to Dad. You'll like his talk," Foxy said.

Looking at his appealing expression, Molly was touched by his championing and intercession. For a twelve-year-old he had an unusual capacity for understanding. "Sure," she tousled his red hair reassuringly, "that'll be fine, and how about your coming camping with me sometime?"

"Golly, YES!"

That evening Foxy chaperoned her gaily through Camp 7 which was up and across the river from 19. "Chummy, aren't they?" He indicated the close-packed tents where canvas nearly met canvas, and campfire smoke drifted between neighboring camps.

Each site was equipped with picnic tables, attached benches, and rocked, metal-topped firesites. Water faucets and trash cans were placed at frequent intervals. Large, modern rest rooms were nearby. People talked, children shouted, radios blared, and cars circled, causing constant noise.

"Ugh," Molly shuddered, remembering Tamarack's

peace. "This isn't camping. It's like living in a city, only worse."

Foxy nodded. "Dad says it's part of the naturalist's job to tell the campers about the fine, high country camps."

Parents sat and children wiggled on benches marching downhill to a log stage hosting a movie screen. "Let's sit in front," Foxy suggested.

She spotted Breck adding wood to a crackling campfire while Irving Dawson mounted the stage and put on a collar microphone. "He's master of ceremonies," Foxy whispered explanation; "he'll make announcements and lead singing before Dad's talk."

A few babies cried and some young wigglers couldn't be kept in their seats, but the large audience sang enthusiastically. Song words to old favorites appeared on the screen after Tim clicked the projector switch in his hand. The participation was fun and friendly, and Molly relaxed.

It was almost dark when Breck was introduced, and she was relieved to see that he talked in the shadows while light pinpointed the color slides illustrating his subject. Campfire talks seemed easier than morning talks because visitors were looking at pictures instead of the speaker.

Breck's topic was the "Four Seasons of Yosemite." The winter slides, especially, drew sighs and spontaneous clapping. His commentary surprised Molly with its dry wit. "Skiing," he remarked, "is a favorite winter sport, even though it has its ups and downs." Accompanying his words was a picture of Foxy falling headlong in a tangle of arms, legs, skis, and poles.

Another time, showing a series of beautiful spring flowers, he commented, "But flowers aren't the only thing that bloom in Yosemite every spring. . . ." A picture flashed on of a child's face pocked with red swellings. "So do mosquitoes and their bites."

Molly laughed aloud. "See!" Foxy stated in a triumphant whisper. "He's good, isn't he?"

"Yes." Her answer reflected surprise and amusement.

After the close of the program, she intended to go down front to congratulate Breck, but it seemed half the audience had the same idea.

"Come on," urged Foxy. "I can use my elbows."

"No, thanks," she shuddered. "Crowds scare me."

"But Dad's waving."

Molly turned to see Breck, still on the stage, beaming and giving a come-on wave. Another look at the people swarming toward him made her shake her head. "Later." Her call was swallowed by crowd noise.

Foxy walked beside her aiming an erratic flashlight at the sky, tree trunks, everywhere except the dimly lighted path. "Dad will think you didn't like him."

"I'll tell him at campfire."

"I wish you'd gone up just then like everybody else." Rebellion was in his tone.

Carefully, she chose words. "I'm not like everybody else. I'm shy of people."

Foxy blurted miserably, "Dad says you're stuck up."

Anger rose in her, but she kept her voice patient. "No, I withdraw and go away, not because I'm stuck up but because crowds, noise, and confusion kind of suffocate me."

"Oh," he said thoughtfully; then added, "Anyway, I wish you and my dad liked each other."

To that loyal cry, she had no answer. Back at camp she changed quickly into jeans and a sweat shirt and hurried out to the woodpile for campfire logs. She had it well-stacked, wood crosswise, before Irving and others joined her. The fire caught and leaped high within seconds after she applied a match.

Breck's sarcastic speech spoiled her pleasure. "On top of everything else, a woodwoman! Did you use flint or two Boy Scouts rubbed together?"

Molly froze. Her intentions of saying something nice about Breck's talk withered icily. She tried to excuse him. Perhaps he had misunderstood her turning away after the talks; maybe he had, but surely Foxy would have told him of her appreciation. There was no reason she could summon to excuse his sarcasm, his embarrassing her publicly.

Oblivious of the chill, Gloria arrived chattering, "If you people aren't sleepy now, my talk on mammals will take care of that. May I practice my new talk on you?"

"Sure." There was immediate, enthusiastic agreement. Irving set up a screen; Dutch and Breck ran an extension cord from a nearby tent and placed a projector on a card table.

Firelight danced and quiet reigned while Gloria gave her illustrated talk. Well back from the listeners' circle, Molly leaned against a tree. Gloria's lecture surprised her with its facts and overall dullness. Her slides were good enough, but there were no lively action shots.

Finished, Gloria resumed her normal vivaciousness. "All right, savages, tear it apart."

"Dull," Dutch commented. "Sorry, gal, but you almost succeeded in putting me to sleep."

Breck was more careful with his criticism. "If you'd check the slide file again for more colorful pictures, say a bear catching a fish or scaring campers, I think you might work in more human interest."

Two others offered enlivening ideas. Silent and wide-eyed, Molly wondered if she would be as open to criticism. Whether or not she would be, she thought the practice run before naturalists was a fine, constructive plan.

"Molly?" Gloria invited. "Here's your chance. I won't be easy on you when your time comes. Chew."

Molly spoke slowly. "Your facts are impressive, but overwhelming. I'd like to see you change them some, spark them up."

"How?" The question was inquiring, not defensive.

"Well, for instance, when you say an adult bear weighs between four hundred and six hundred pounds, why not add something like, 'A bear does not watch his weight or worry about the cholesterol level; in fact, his diet isn't particularly selective—he'll eat anything from mice to tomatoes, can and all.' You can think of something better than that, but put in some humor."

"Thanks, coach," Gloria commented warmly. "I'll try."

Breck advised, "Give your listeners facts, pictures, and memories."

"Men that invade these mountains should be sent home with mountain memories," Dutch spoke quietly.

Suspiciously, Gloria queried, "Is that a Muir quote?"

"No, it's a Vanderbunt original, but I do have a quote by a man named Sabin that's in one of our training manuals. He described campfires aptly, 'But see—a spark, a flame, and now The Wilderness is home.' "

"Nice," Tim commented. "True; and to carry it a step farther, an organized campfire led by a naturalist should relate and integrate the wilderness so that it is familiar to the visitor."

"And in so doing," Breck added, "put in a few licks for conservation and the National Park Service. Most of us do that unconsciously because our love for the forests and unspoiled land shows in our words."

There was more good talk on the campfire tradition, its sociability, leadership, suitable subjects, and visitor participation. Molly was impressed. A campfire program was a challenge, and she wondered if she could come up with one enriching enough so that visitors would have new ideas and better understanding of Yosemite.

Their campfire was falling into glowing embers that mesmerized her. Moving forward, she sat Indian-style and Indian-quiet, but with the others, feeling a kinship, a belonging to Camp 19 that surprised and pleased her.

"Coming after tumultuous day," Dutch's voice was soft, "night is blessed, cool and still with lonely stars and lonelier thoughts."

Yawns, a general scrambling upward announced campfire's end. Molly stood, tall with thoughts. "Muir?"

Dutch was shoveling the coals over with dirt. "No, mine."

Molly noted his hesitation, his evident shyness, and wanted to say something complimentary yet individual. He looked so hard, so unyielding; yet he saw and expressed beauty softly, memorably.

Inadequately, she mumbled, "Thanks for the thoughts."

The next day Molly answered literally hundreds of questions at the information desk with ease and charity. When a visitor was rude and complaining, she reminded herself that a flat tire, a poor campsite, even mosquito bites might have influenced his mood. When someone asked, "Where am I?" she tried to orient him with map consultation and cheerful words. Her own buoyancy was caused by the thought of being a uniformed NPS representative, and that Junior Rangers would begin the following day, releasing her from desk duty.

Her reading and training were paying off in ready answers to queries on roads, trails, wildlife, and diverse other subjects. Toward quitting time, her public manner was fading, her mind rebelling; but her speech remained low, courteous, and informative until a brash young man in his early twenties saluted her smartly.

"So the Marines even have a beachhead in Yosemite!" he whistled. "Tell me, madam sir, what do you know of the wildlife here? Do you know a bear from a wolf?"

Visitors laughed and crowded closer to hear her answer. Out of the corner of her eye, she saw Dutch standing by the drinking fountain, face frozen. Unamused, but good-humored, she replied, "Each summer Yosemite has a two-legged wolf population."

"Ah," her annoyer persisted, "it's a wise girl who

knows her wolves. How many four-legged specimens roam this place?"

"None," she assured him, glad to be thrown a reasonable question. "No wolf has ever been sighted in this area."

He grinned. "Until now! How about foxes? I bet you see some foxy characters around here."

"Yes," her agreement was formal and factual. "Park visitors may see the Townsend gray fox and occasionally the red fox."

"Oh, thanks a lot." His smartness subsided, but he kept asking her questions about wildlife.

She answered easily, feeling proud of the knowledge stored in her brain.

"Say, can I take the Coulterville Road to Merced Grove?"

Instantly, the place names associated themselves with history; an 1874 stagecoach route and a little-known grove of giant sequoias. "That road was abandoned years ago," she replied casually.

"Can't I drive some of it? My car is a species of mountain goat."

"Sorry," she said firmly. "You might try hiking it, but car travel is impossible."

Dutch moved up. "Miss Bishop is misinformed. The road is open clear to Coulterville, though in dusty, rutty state. Step over here, and I can show you on the map."

Molly's cheeks flamed; more so, moments later, when Dutch returned, leaned over the desk and advised quietly, "Don't ever be a nature faker. If you don't know the answers, call upstairs to someone who does."

Whatever else he was going to say was silenced by a carrot-topped girl crying, "I want my mommy. Where is she?"

Dutch hunched down on his heels facing the distraught child. "I bet I could help you find her. Where did you see her last?"

"Out there." The girl pointed toward the wild flower garden. "But now she's gone, and I need her!"

"Of course," Dutch assured her. "Let's take a walk and see if we can find her."

Still embarrassed by his rightful rebuke of her, Molly watched his courtesy and grave friendliness with the girl, wondering if he'd be glacial with her from then on. He had looked so cold, so forbidding when he had made the "nature faker" crack, and, she reminded herself, he had been so right.

When Molly entered the tent, still downcast and vaguely antagonistic toward mankind, Laura called cheerily, "Dinner in fifteen minutes. We're having steaks. My treat. I thought it would be nice to dine together and have a little sociability."

"Sorry," Molly said curtly. "I'm not in the mood." Shoulders slumped, she walked in the back tent and changed clothes hurriedly. Her corner was neat, spartan with two garment bags, a small mirror, and a shelf holding hand cream, deodorant, and a bottle of perfume. Gloria had board shelving along six feet of the tent side covered with jars, bottles, boxes, powder puffs, atomizers, eyebrow pencil, two full lipstick caddies, a portable hair dryer, and every other conceivable beauty aid.

Facing this array across the tent was Laura's spread

of feminine aids beside a large, full-length mirror. The mirror's wood frame held snapshots of her Pekinese dog, and her nondescript city apartment.

Molly looked at the cluttered tent in distaste, wishing that she had one to herself. Sociability, women, frills —the artificiality revolted her. Grabbing a towel she escaped both tents. Laura's back was to her as she stirred onions in a savory smelling concoction in her electric frying pan. As she shoved open the screen door, Molly said again, "Sorry, Laura."

The older woman said, "Never mind. I should have remembered the adage about the mule."

On her way downriver to swim, Molly pondered that remark; finally, angrily, she recalled her father's admonishing, "If a mule kicks you once, shame on him. If he kicks you twice, shame on you."

Laura's analogy annoyed yet shamed her, but togetherness in her depressed state had seemed torturous. A vigorous swim and a brisk walk should restore her humor and perspective.

After doing splashing violence to the placid river, running along it to warm herself, and lying in the dying sun, she ran to camp feeling vibrant, hungry, and human.

"Hi," she greeted Gloria, who was drying dishes. "Where's Laura?"

"At the movie. Do you care?"

"Not really." Molly was puzzled at Gloria's sarcasm. "I was just asking to be polite."

"It's a little late to remember your manners," Gloria commented coolly. "I wish you had observed them earlier before you hurt Laura's feelings. She was crying."

Molly felt defensive, childlike. "I told her I was sorry. I wish she'd learn that I like being alone."

Cuttingly, Gloria interrupted, "She has *now;* the rest of us knew when you skipped the potluck. After this, though, please don't take your growing up out on Laura."

Red seeped into her cheeks as Molly followed Gloria into the back tent. "What do you mean by that? I am grown up; I'm nineteen, almost twenty."

Gloria scowled at her mirrored reflection as she adjusted her airline-hostess-type hat, applied lipstick, and brushed on some powder. "Molly, I told you the other night that your attitude is immature. You refuse to give or join in camp life, yet you are hurt and defensive when criticized. I am sorry to be so clinical, but you are so antisocial."

Molly stood silent, feeling grossly misunderstood and rebellious.

Gloria said briskly, "Lecture's over. If you are going to hear Dale Hudson talk on Yosemite history at Yosemite Lodge, you better do a quick change."

Resentfully, Molly demanded, "Is it a command performance?"

"Not really; but most of us attend because he's Chief Park Naturalist, an authority on area history, and an excellent speaker. You might learn something."

Molly remembered her lack of knowledge on the Coulterville Road. "I'll go. Do I have to wear my uniform? Won't I be right in jeans? At that, I'm better dressed than most Park visitors in their shorts and slacks.

Gloria said, "But you aren't a visitor!"

Thoughtfully, Molly pulled off her bathing suit and

began to dress. Not only had Gloria accused her of being immature, but had implied that she had little respect for the Park Service. Mentally, she snorted, baloney—her uniform enlarged her pride, much as a fluttering American flag stirred her. She didn't mind the stares and looks of respect it earned her.

As she bicycled down the path to the bridge that would take her to the Lodge, she chewed Gloria's words, and a chocolate bar.

Toward the close of Dale's interesting slide-illustrated talk, Tim McCorkle slid in beside her on the last bench and her stomach began to complain of hunger. Its rumbling worried her, but Tim seemed intent on Dale's final words. As applause swelled up and people began to leave, his eyes swept her neat appearance.

"Nice," he approved, smiling. "Official yet lady-like."

"Thanks." She was glad Gloria had goaded her into wearing her uniform. "Care for a cup of coffee, Ranger?" Tim invited.

As if in answer, her stomach growled audibly. Color suffused her face, and embarrassment throttled speech.

Tim's eyes lit up, his mouth twitched. Another rumble undid him. Laughter burst out until Molly couldn't help joining him.

"As you can tell," she chuckled, "I haven't had dinner. Where's the nearest hamburger? Coffee wouldn't do much for me right now."

"Follow me to a chocolate malt." He took her hand and led her into the Lodge coffee shop; teasing, "Most of my dates are on diets; you're likely to cost me money."

Over two hamburgers, french fries and malts for both, he told her he was a forestry major at the Davis campus of the University of California. He loved horseback riding, flying, jazz, and girls, preferably brunettes. "Now tell me about you. From camp I know you're shy, independent, a good horseshoe player, and smart," he said.

She bent over her malt, newly embarrassed. So she had the reputation of being independent and smart! Unsuitable replies circled in her head.

"What do you like to do?" he rescued her. "Besides eat?"

"Hike, explore, read, swim, ride. I like just about any outdoors thing. I like nature and knowing about it." She checked his expression for amusement or sarcasm, found none, and continued, "I'm not really intellectual, but I've learned a lot of natural sciences because they fascinate me. I like solitude and space and—golly—I'm talking too much."

"No, you're not." He stood up, took her hand again, paid the check and led her out. "I've been wanting to know more about you. Let's do this again—soon."

CHAPTER V

Before she left for Junior Rangers the next day, Molly attempted to make amends to Laura. Her unexpected date with Tim, their talking, rapport, and the warm way he had said, "Let's do this again—soon," had put her in a buoyant mood. She apologized for coming in late, asked if the movie had been good and who had won the baseball game. Laura answered in stiff monosyllables that disturbed Molly's lightheartedness. Gloria's understanding, grateful smile sustained her though Laura remained hurt and uncommunicative. She and Gloria breakfasted lightly on tea and coffee, respectively; while Molly enjoyed bacon, fried eggs, toast, and a fresh peach.

"Revolting." Gloria pointed at the jam-heaped toast. "Food at this ungodly hour in the morning. Ugh! And why aren't you in bed? Laura and I have to be at work by eight, but Junior Rangers doesn't begin until nine."

Sunnily, Molly confessed, "I was up at six, making

track casts back of camp. I got some clear prints."

Instantly, Gloria was alert. "What kind? Bear, deer, and raccoons, I suppose. Anything else?"

"A fox, I think. It left a small track similar to a coyote's pawprint."

"Probably a gray fox," Gloria said interestedly. "I don't have time to look at your cast now, but I heard a couple of hoarse 'rawk' barks back of camp last night. That very well could have been a fox, nosing around for berries and field mice. Good tracking, gal; I want to see them tonight. Come on, Laura."

Molly watched them go, freshly amazed at Gloria who was so knowledgeable, so sure of nature, yet never betrayed her brains by appearing anything but wholly feminine and yielding out of uniform. Maybe she could take lessons and absorb some of the other girl's poise and sweetness.

Gathering bacon, eggs, and milk, she returned them to the cold bear baffle and was heading for the parking lot when she heard Betty Fox exclaim, "That girl! Will she ever remember?"

"Me?"

Betty was by the washtubs, her arms full of dirty clothes, expression angry. "No, Gloria! Look, she's had lingerie soaking in this tub for two days. Honestly, there are other people in camp who might like to use it."

"She's been so busy she forgot," Molly defended her friend. "Here, I'll take it out." So Molly, whose own plain cotton underwear was always consigned to a washing machine, carefully rinsed Gloria's sheer, lacy black things before hanging them to dry.

Betty watched Molly's domesticity in surprised silence until a "Don't wring them so hard" plea that seemed forced out of her at the sight of lace being vigorously manhandled.

Even with the delay, Molly arrived at the Happy Isles Nature Center forty-five minutes ahead of time. Breck and Irving were there too, arranging supplies on picnic tables that were placed at scattered areas on clear, flat land. A low rail fence separated the Junior Ranger "campus" from the rest of the Nature Center; alders, dogwood, oaks, and maples encircled the other three sides. Glacier Point towered to the south; farther northeast Half Dome's bulk blocked the sun. Molly shivered, wishing she had a long-sleeved uniform shirt like the men's instead of her short-sleeved white blouse.

Irving noted her coldness. "After the sun climbs over the mountain, you'll be wishing for some of this shade. At Junior Rangers, we either freeze or fry. Would you carry a stack of color books over to the bear table, please?"

She remembered from her training that attending children were divided into three age groups. The Bear group included twelve- and thirteen-year-olds; the Deer group, ten- and eleven-year-olds; and the Chipmunks were composed of youngsters eight and nine. Each group had its own work tables, supervised by a Ranger-naturalist.

"Which group will I be with?" she asked Breck, who was setting up a registration table.

"Chipmunks this morning," he answered impersonally. "We trade around, but your counseling experience should especially suit you to guide the younger ages."

He loomed big, calm, competent, but unsympathetic to Molly, who knew that as ranger-naturalist in charge, he would be her boss for the following eight weeks. "That's fine," she replied evenly. "I like them any age."

"Remember," he advised heavily, "keep your lecturing to a minimum and encourage thinking discussion. For example, when you're displaying reptiles, have your group discover by touch and observation how and what a snake eats, what good he does, where he lives, and his relationship to his environment. We try to stress ecology, as our Junior Rangers can relate that to home, whether home is in Maine, Oklahoma, or California."

Breck's continued lecture duplicated her training, but Molly listened politely and attentively until warmly bundled children started streaming in. Breck had her help register them. Some had freshly combed, water-slicked-back hair; others sleep in their eyes and bits of breakfast on their chins. Nine o'clock was early for campers, Molly knew, for parents had to contend with unusual living conditions, smoky wood campfires, and a natural reluctance not to leave sleeping bags before the sun fingered treetops.

Easily, she elicited information from registrants. "I bet you're twelve, so you'll be in the Bear group. How many days will you be coming to Junior Rangers?"

"Five, if it isn't like school," a snub-nosed girl confided, grinning. "I'm sick of school."

"Me, too," Molly replied, "but this program is very different. I'll label your name tag 'Bear—5 days,' and now I need your name."

"Sandra Lee Smith,—that's L-e-e," she said.

Carefully, Molly printed "Sandra S.," pinned the tag to the girl and asked, "Do you have a quarter? That's the daily charge to cover the price of supplies."

Boys and girls moved past her in jeans and hooded sweat shirts. Her own arms prickled with goose bumps, reminding her to wear her uniform jacket other mornings.

The children were shiny-eyed with anticipation, and important with wonder imparted after her questions.

"So you're in Camp 14. Seen any bear?"

"Golly, yes! One knocks over the garbage can about ten times a night. A huge one."

A badly sunburned girl gave Molly a clue. "Were you hiking yesterday?"

"Clear up to the top of Yosemite Falls, that's all! Have you ever been on that trail? It's kinda scary, but fun, and you should see the view. You can see for miles and miles."

"I saw the Mariposa Grove of giant sequoias," a carrot-headed boy tried to top her. "They're so tall you can't even see the tops, and they're older than anything. Those crazy trees were growing before people had electricity; even way before Columbus discovered America!"

"Right." Molly pinned on his name tag, thinking that such youngsters were ripe for fully appreciating the wonder and fragility of the out-of-doors. Junior Rangers had been organized in 1930, under a different name, for the same purpose she would help carry out; to teach the values of nature and train youngsters to treasure what they found exciting and beautiful. Through this training would develop conservation-minded adults who would help protect all natural parks.

One stocky boy announced, "I'll be eight next month. I can be a Junior Ranger, can't I?"

"I guess so." Molly smiled at his earnestness.

Breck overheard. "Sorry," he said curtly, "eight to thirteen are our age limits. No exceptions."

Tears welled in the boy's eyes. "But I'm almost eight, and will be in third grade next fall."

"Sorry. Come back next year."

The boy left crying. Breck shrugged. "You see, my dear, second-graders are too immature."

Molly's eyes blazed, but she returned silently to her task. Probably the rule was good, needed, yet that eager boy could surely have been an exception. Soon she turned two more underage applicants away with sympathetic, explaining words. It seemed Breck had no rapport with children. Why was he leading this program?

Once the forty-three youngsters were seated on logs around the campfire circle, Breck became a different person; easy, slow-talking, and appealing. "Hello, down there," he used his six-foot-four-inch height for a laugh. "I'm Ranger-naturalist Breck and while Ranger Irving over there registers latecomers, let's have a little get-acquainted singing. Who knows 'John Jacob Jingleheimer Schmidt'? Good, let's go."

After that he led them in "The More We Get Together" with some original verses applicable to Yosemite. Then the enthusiastic singers chose several songs; finally, Breck taught them "The Mosquito Song" to the tune of "Tramp, Tramp, the Boys Are Marching." They

stomped their feet, and clapped their hands, and sang
loudly:

> Snap, snap, the mosquitoes are biting.
> Cheer up, comrades, I have four;
> And beneath my fingernails
> I shall squash their little tails
> Till they promise not to bite me any more.

From there on the children were his to command,
but he did it so gently that Molly was impressed. "If you
Junior Rangers can stick around for five days, I think you
will learn a lot about conservation, the relationship of
living things to one another, mammals, birds, and trees.
If we ranger-naturalists think you are qualified, those of
you who can attend only three days will be awarded
badges. Anyone who comes five days and can recite the
conservation pledge will be awarded a Junior Ranger
patch. Let's see, is there a last year's graduate in the
crowd? Fine, come up here, please, and show off your
patch."

A pig-tailed girl, aglow with self-conscious pride,
showed her big sewed-on patch with Half Dome above
the words "Junior Ranger."

"That could be your tangible award," Breck spoke
quietly, "but the intangible rewards—things you can't
touch or see—will be an appreciation and knowledge of
Yosemite. I want you to memorize the conservation
pledge and make it part of your life. Repeat after me, 'I
give my pledge as an American to save and faithfully

defend from waste the natural resources of my country —its soil and minerals, its forests, waters, and wildlife.' "

Along with the serious children, Molly, too, felt a thrill and a promise in saying the pledged words. It was like a prayer.

Breck smiled in the sudden silence after the pledge. "Now, I'll give you some other homework. See how many of you can find out the highest waterfall and the highest mountain in Yosemite and tell me the answers tomorrow. By the way, you don't have to climb up and measure; the answers are given on signs, in booklets, and in the museum.

"Our learning week begins this morning with a study of mammals; tomorrow we find out about trees and plants; Wednesday, birds; Thursday, reptiles; and Friday, a general review and awarding of patches. Later, I'll tell you about a couple of afternoon programs on Indians, fire and search and rescue. Now, to your tables; all Bear over there, Deer back here, and Chipmunks by the rail fence with Ranger Molly."

The sun blazed over the mountain, making Molly glad that the Chipmunk tables were shaded by alder trees. Sixteen eager faces looked to her for guidance. At ease, she began, "Who knows what a mammal is?"

Answers were immediate and varied. She waved to a tall boy name-tagged Roger to reply for all. "I'm a mammal," he explained; "so are you, so's an elephant, or a bear."

"Is there a common characteristic of all mammals?" she asked.

Two youngsters put an end to the guesses by saying

almost in unison, "All mammals give milk to their young."

"Right," Molly said, "so man, horses, even rats, are related. Pretty soon we will go on a walk to observe signs of mammals. If we are quiet, we might see some Yosemite mammals. What do you think we might find?"

This time the answers were less wild. "Squirrels." "Deer." "Maybe a bear."

Molly was pleased to be on the asking, instead of receiving, end of questions and tried to gear her queries so that the children would think before bursting into speech. Just before they left for the nature walk, she asked, "Who knows about trail safety? What are the rules?"

"Stay on the trail." "Stay together." "Don't take shortcuts." "Pick up your feet so you won't make dust."

Their lively, intelligent responses carried out on a trail that led through forest, through meadows, and along the river. Molly felt a secure sense of well-bing, a belonging that she had not experienced before in Yosemite.

The meadow was tall with green grass and wild flowers full in the sun. Jackets and shirts were shed and tied around thin waists, eyes darted everywhere, and voices were hushed.

"See that blue flower, Ranger? That's a lupine, isn't it? Did the Indians eat that?"

"No, but come over here and look at this manzanita bush. The Indians ate these small berries. Does anyone know what *manzanita* means in English?"

Three Spanish-learning children chorused, "Little apple."

A boy scowled with thought. "Maybe the Indians

made apple cider with those berries. Do you think?"

"They certainly did, and the berries were eaten raw too. Now let's walk through the meadow on the trail. Why should we be especially careful to keep on the trail here?"

"Because we might trample the grass so it wouldn't be pretty."

"That's one reason. Who can think of another?"

A boy suggested, "Our big feet might trample an animal's hole or step on some bird eggs."

"Here's a hole right beside the trail." Molly knelt down to part the concealing grass. "Who do you suppose lives in that hole? What does he eat and do? How do you suppose this meadow was formed?"

By the end of a half hour, she could see even the shy children grappling with ideas and giving thoughtful answers. They were fortunate enough to observe several birds, chattering squirrels, and one antlered buck.

Upon their return to the work tables, she led more discussion; then set them to coloring the deer pictured in the special Junior Ranger color books. Time sped by until a final gathering around the campfire circle, a last song, and dismissal at eleven-thirty.

Breck led that. "Let's give a yell that will be heard at Glacier Point," he invited, "like this: 1—2—3, CLASS DISMISSED! All together now."

Molly yelled too and laughed at the resounding result. Children charged off to waiting parents, but she wasn't free. Several brought parents back to meet her, and one girl appealed, "Will you be in a picture with me?"

She posed gladly, feeling useful and happy after the stimulating session. Irving teased, "No one ever wants me to be in a picture. What do you have that I don't?"

Even Breck unbent some. "Enjoy your morning?"

"Oh yes, immensely! And you're good with songs and children." For once, spontaneity prompted whole-hearted praise.

"Why, thanks," he smiled slowly, and she saw that his homeliness could be pleasant. "I'm glad you found something about me to approve."

"Very much." She let the sarcasm pass; then hurried to put things away.

Breck made another overture. "How about a ride home? You can stuff your bicycle in my station wagon."

"No, thanks," she disappointed him. "I have my bathing suit with me, and I'm going to use my two hours off in the river."

He nodded. "I keep forgetting how irresponsible you are."

She bristled, "What do you mean by that? I do my jobs and was only late that once."

"I didn't mean irresponsible in that sense. You misunderstand me. I meant you're not responsible for definite meal hours, kids, and a wife."

Molly pedaled away unconvinced. Nothing she did ever pleased the big ranger, and very little he said or did satisfied her.

Gloria accused her of being immature, Dutch thought she was superior, and now Breck labeled her irresponsible. She sighed. Thank goodness *she wasn't* tied down to a family with attendant responsibilities. Maybe she would stay single forever to keep her freedom, the independence that allowed swimming and sunning when other women were tied to clocks and children's hunger pangs.

As she wheeled her bike away from the popular Nature Center, away from people, noise, and the abrasiveness of confusion, she reflected that such a single state might well be labeled selfish by others. Perhaps she was; but surely teaching, also in her planned future, was unselfish, a giving of herself that should satisfy any obligation to society?

She frowned. Such bothering, worrying thoughts had never entered her mind until the interdependent living demanded by community life in Camp 19. If she could hibernate in the woods by herself and come out only for Junior Rangers. . . .

Despite her longing to be a hermit, Molly spent a fairly social evening showing her dried track casts to Gloria and Foxy, playing horseshoes with Tim, and discussing Junior Rangers with Irving outside his tent.

"Come on over to Breck's tent," he invited, "and help us settle the affairs of Yosemite."

"No, thanks," she answered quickly. "I want to do some reading on trees before tomorrow morning's nature walk."

"Gloria and Laura will be coming," he urged.

"I know," she chuckled, "and that's exactly why I am staying home. When Laura's gone, the baseball game's off, and I can concentrate."

"You have a point there, but you know you're not helping your reputation as being antisocial."

"I don't care," she shrugged, secretly pleased that Irving did. As she sauntered home, she wondered if Tim and Dutch would be in Breck's tent, if they would care that she wasn't.

Later, her reading done, the gusts of laughter and the aroma of coffee intrigued her; but how could she back down on her renowned antisocialness then?

Next morning she thought of an olive branch and offered it to an unsmiling Breck. "I wondered if Foxy couldn't attend Junior Rangers again as sort of a helper? You know, helping with name tags, passing out color books—that kind of thing."

She imagined she could see him mentally sifting her suggestion for an ulterior motive. "Never mind," she added, ready to flee, "it was just an idea."

"Wait a minute," he boomed. "Don't be so touchy. It's a good idea. Brewster will probably think it's the best one he's ever heard. As a matter of fact, we always ask some older youngsters to give us a hand. Come in, come in, join us for a final cup of coffee."

"No, thanks." She was almost sorry to refuse as she saw disapproval regain his face.

"Why on earth not? Are you afraid of wasting ten minutes?"

"No, no." This time she cleared up the new misunderstanding by confessing defensively, "I don't drink coffee."

Jovially, he opened the screen door, commenting, "I suppose you're too young? How about milk or cocoa?" He raised his already-booming voice. "Brewster, there's a lady to see you."

Unlike mammals, trees were solid and easy to find on that morning's nature walk. Molly's Chipmunk group, with an important Foxy herding stragglers, observed six different kinds. "What do these trees do that's important to the soil?" she asked, standing at the thickly pine-needled foot of a large Jeffrey pine.

"Fertilize it with pine needles?" A child scuffed them with her foot, forehead knotted briefly. "No, that's wrong; I bet the needles help build up the ground."

Another girl added, "The tree's roots help the soil to hold water. Then rain can't wash the ground away."

"Yes, and the trees give us shade."

"What about the bark? What good does it do?" Molly asked.

"It's the tree's skin. It protects the tree from being hurt."

"Yes." Molly was pleased at the thinking behind the answers. "What good does the bark do after it falls off?"

"Well, it falls apart. . . ."

"Decays?" she suggested.

"Yeah, decays and that's good for the soil."

She had the children hold their noses close to the bark crevices. "What do you smell?"

"Pineapple. Vanilla. No, pineapple, um . . . good!"

"Either one," she agreed. "You can always tell a Jeffrey pine by that distinctive odor. Now let's look at its cone."

Again the morning went too fast for her, and she was satisfied she had done a thorough job of stirring naturalist thinking. Tim had charge of the Deer group

78

and, from the laughter, kept them entertained as well as interested. One overheard exchange showed her why he was so popular.

A youngster kicked at a wooden box containing an underground faucet. "What's that?"

"That's a submarine," Tim responded lightly, "and though this isn't reptile day, I'll give you some advance information: that long green thing stretched out on the ground is a water snake."

Molly envied his sense of the ridiculous but found her own light touch hugely enjoyed in a song just before dismissal. She taught them:

I stuck my head in a little skunk's hole
And the little skunk said, "Well, bless my soul.
Take it out! Take it out! REMOVE IT! ! !"

I *didn't* take it out and the little skunk said,
"If you *don't* take it out you'll wish you were *dead.*
Take it out! *Take it out!*" PHEWIE! I *removed* it!

"Very good," Tim complimented immediately after the dismissal yell. "That's a new one to me. How about lunching with a nonsmelling ranger? I just happen to know a far-from-intimate, big not little, populated not uncrowded cafeteria where we can buy food not ambrosia."

Eyes dancing, she countered, "I just happen to know

a maid and a boy who are going to escape the maddening crowd by lunching on the river out of a big, sack lunch. Care to join us instead?"

"Peanut butter and jelly sandwiches for a growing boy?" he teased, but she could see he was pleased at the idea.

"Even baloney and cheese sandwiches for a growing girl," she countered. "Come on."

That afternoon Molly was scheduled to attend the Indian program for Junior Rangers. Since the audience would be mainly children and she had given the Indian talk three afternoons at the museum, she assumed she would do the speaking. Her confidence was bolstered enough so that she didn't dread the experience at all; in fact, she anticipated sharing her knowledge and collected Indian artifacts with her Junior Ranger friends.

Whistling, she carried her things from the bicycle basket to the campfire circle.

Breck hustled over and, misunderstanding, commented, "Excellent examples of arrowheads. Thanks for bringing them. I'll use them to illustrate part of my talk."

"I thought I was to talk," she blurted. "After all, I've been giving the Indian story every afternoon lately, and that's been my specialty down south."

Breck stared at her coldly, mimicking sarcastically, "After all, I know a few facts about Indians too. Maybe I'm not an authority, but my talks have been well received in the past."

Molly recoiled from his irony. Her impulsiveness had antagonized him just as a tentative rapport had been established. As children, many accompanied by parents, streamed in, she carried most of her artifacts to a work table and then leaned against a tree, embarrassed and resentful.

Though she listened critically to Breck, she found his talk factual and enjoyable. At the end he showed her mounted arrowheads, pointing out their perfectness. "Yosemite Indians," he added, "excelled at two things not known or needed now. These were basketweaving and arrowhead making."

An adult's hand shot up. "Ranger, how did they make arrowheads? I know they used obsidian, but how were the arrowheads fashioned?"

"Simply by breaking the obsidian, which is a glass-like volcanic rock into workable pieces, then shaping a chosen piece with a piece of deer antler." Breck smiled. "A lively, if deadly art in the olden, golden days; now a lost art."

A teen-ager inquired, "Doesn't anyone make them any more?"

"Baskets, yes," Breck answered. "Here in the Valley we have Julia Parker, a skilled Indian woman, who will start demonstrating basketweaving next week. As for arrowhead making, I know of no one who knows how."

Briefly Molly wrestled with her inhibitions, but the audience appeared so interested that she stepped forward to volunteer in a small voice, "I do."

Breck responded, "I should have known! Do you, by any remote chance, have your tools with you?"

She ignored the sarcasm that the audience construed as teasing. "Yes, right back here."

"Then," Breck announced, "I'll adjourn the formal part of the program, and those of you who wish may watch Ranger Molly Bishop demonstrate arrowhead making."

Half the audience crowded around Molly, who sat on the table so all could see. Momentarily, the mass of people frightened her, but the many familiar faces of children stopped that.

"For tools," she exhibited her own, "Indian men used points off deer antlers in one hand, like this, to chip away at the obsidian held in the other hand, like this. As they did, I use a piece of buckskin to protect my hand against the sharp, volcanic glass.

"An old Indian chief in the San Bernardino mountains taught me how to shape arrowheads slowly and patiently."

An awed boy asked, "How long does it take to make just one?"

"About a half hour of steady work," she explained. "A spear point takes much longer." Although her watchers were respectful, she was aware of Breck standing by, arms crossed, expression veiled.

She realized that, once more, she had given him cause to think her a show-off.

CHAPTER VI

That evening she audited a campfire talk given by Dutch on "Men of Yosemite." He spoke of Chief Tenaya, James Savage, James Hutchings, Galen Clark, John Muir, and President Theodore Roosevelt "who, though only a brief visitor to Yosemite in 1903, was inspired by its unique surroundings, Muir's persuasiveness, and his own appreciation of the importance of conservation. President Roosevelt used all in his official powers to see that conservation became a national cause."

For illustrations he showed black-and-white slides, reproduced photographs, that lent depth and authenticity to human history.

Afterward Dutch called, "I'll walk home with you."

Because she had to push her bicycle beside her, the walk was a little complicated, and his first remark confirmed her suspicions of Breck.

"I hear you're an expert on making arrowheads."

Vocally she cringed, "I know how."

"That's grand. Would you show me? I had thought you didn't care for human history, just nature history."

His obvious interest encouraged her into explanation. "You see, the camp where I spent every summer was near an Indian reservation. An old chief talked to us occasionally, and I used to go see him. Gradually he taught me lore, legend, and skills. He even gave me an Indian name—Girl-Who-Asks-Questions."

"Is Monday your day off?" Dutch asked. "Good. Tim and I are going botanizing along the old Coulterville Road, and we thought you might like to come along."

Delighted, she said, "It's a deal. I'll make lunch. As a Muir follower, do you live on raisins and nuts?"

He laughed, "That diet's fine *if* you add sandwiches, fruit, and cookies to it."

After she showed him all her Indian artifacts, he spoiled the evening by saying, "Let's join the others in Breck's tent."

"Not tonight," she answered. "I'm tired."

"Sure?" Grave, glacial eyes questioned her sincerity before he walked quietly out of the tent door.

"Sure," she called after him, half-truthfully. If it hadn't been for the expected sarcasm from Breck, she would have accompanied Dutch. Amused, she realized that he hadn't quoted Muir once during their meeting. She wandered into the bedroom tent and, uncharacteristically, studied herself in Laura's full-length mirror.

The reflected image showed a casualness that amounted to carelessness, from the wrinkled shirtmaker dress with its torn pocket to her auburn hair. It was uncombed, her worn lipstick had been applied crookedly, and her nose was shiny. If Mother could see me now, Molly thought critically, she'd disown me. Yet Tim and Dutch had sought her out.

She grimaced, maybe her mother was right; maybe she should take an interest in her looks—not because of what others might think, but for her own satisfaction.

Like a whirlwind she tore into her clothes hamper, yanked out a pile of unironed clothes, set up Gloria's board and began to iron. Sounds wafted to her: laughter from Breck's tent, a child crying, faint breeze, an owl, crickets, and gravel-throated frogs.

Gloria came in dropping evening jacket, bag, and kicking off high heels. "Hello! You still up and being dum-mess-tic! Wonders never cease!" She watched Molly's efficient ironing, then caroled, "Lucky girl, I have just chosen you out of hordes of applicants to be my ironer. "Seriously, I'll be glad to pay you."

"Thanks, I don't need money."

"No wonder, you never spend any. That Lodge dress shop is the undoing of my paycheck. Don't you ever buy things?"

Molly laughed. "A bookstore magnetizes my wallet the way a dress shop does yours. Show me a book, microscope, binoculars, or other nature aids, and I'm broke."

Gloria pursed her mouth and cocked her pretty head. "Now, don't throw that iron at me, but a few dollars spent on yourself would do wonders. For example, a bright silk scarf to brighten up your tailored dresses, a darker shade of lipstick put on a little more carefully and a trifle more frequently, and a new hairdo. . . ."

Molly cast a sidelong look at the mirror, shook her

hair back and said tentatively, "I've been thinking of having my hair cut."

"Gloria's eyes lit decisively. "Sort of a cap around your face with just a hint of bangs. I could do it."

"When? I work tomorrow."

"So do I, silly. Let me find my scissors, and I'll do it right now."

Molly felt hesitant. "Will it be easy to take care of? I *hate* wasting time on my hair."

"I've noticed," the older girl commented drily. "Turn that iron off and tie this towel around your neck. Don't worry, a comb used *at regular intervals,* and a few pin curls some nights will keep you beautiful."

After twenty minutes of careful cutting, thinning, and shaping, she said in a pleased tone, "There, my pretty maid, how's that for a transformation? Don't let it go to your head, but you are a mighty attractive gal!"

"Stop kidding," Molly muttered, embarrassed, but the mirrored image showed a vivacious, bright-eyed girl with pretty, short hair and a quirk to her wide mouth.

While Gloria marched off for a shower, Molly swept up the mess, put the ironing board away in the front tent, and stole frequent surprised looks at herself in the mirror.

Laura bustled in. "Whew, I'm dead. These late nights are too much for an old maid like me. Why, Molly, look at you! You're pretty as can be!"

Molly confided, "Gloria cut my hair."

"Let me see the back. That hairdo has altered your whole appearance. Wait, somewhere here in my drawer I have just the scarf to accent your gray eyes."

So Molly stood aimlessly by while Laura, whom she

had hurt and resented, even laughed at, rummaged to find a gauzy turquoise scarf that was just right. She couldn't find any words except "Thank you," but their sincerity seemed to reach Laura.

Just then Gloria entered, inviting, "Ice cream is on."

Touched by what she thought of as undeserved friendship, Molly spooned vanilla ice cream topped with nuts and chocolate in companionable silence.

Next morning Steller jays awoke her at dawn, and a tree squirrel showered down pieces of a pine cone it was nibbling in a treetop above her. How could anyone sleep with nature inviting everyone to stir, explore, and enjoy an awakening world? As she wondered, she pulled on jeans and sweat shirt, ran a surprised hand over her forgotten shorn hair, and cast a wistful look toward the talus slope back of camp.

Instead of walking that way, she entered the front tent quietly, retrieved the iron, ironing board, and an extension cord which she rigged up near the campfire site. Finding Gloria's clothes was simple. An untidy pile sat in a chair just inside the door, and several dresses hung on the line where they had been for two days.

Molly marveled, as she dampened things, how Gloria could appear always trim, bandbox-neat, yet be so careless, with everything she owned. Her outgiving self and generosity overshadowed such faults.

Camp 19 began stirring. Molly heard alarm clocks; voices muttered, stove lids clanged, hatchets split kindling, a baby howled, and the door to the bear baffle thumped repeatedly as food-seekers entered and departed.

All was hushed in their tent. It was Laura's day off and Gloria was dutyless until ten. Sun filtering through trees reminded Molly that, this being Saturday with no Junior Rangers, she was due for desk duty at eight. Ordinarily she would have stormed in to make breakfast, but the memory of the night's kindness made her tiptoe in to change into her uniform.

Having decided to buy breakfast, she jumped into her car to save time. The engine caught, coughed, and stopped twice before she threw back the hood to investigate.

Breck joined her to peer in. "I'll be glad to look at this later. Meanwhile, want a ride?" His expression was passive, his speech impersonal, yet she felt another truce was being offered.

"Yes, please," she answered quickly, spontaneously. "It's too late now to ride my bike." On the way she said nothing about breakfast, figuring to have time to run for a snack after they arrived at the museum. Unknowing, Breck stopped twice, once for gas and once for a picture.

"Isn't that buck a beauty? Mind if I take a picture?"

"Of course not." She didn't mind, but her stomach did. It rumbled so fiercely, so embarrassingly, that Breck noticed after he reentered the station wagon.

"What's that noise? No breakfast? If you lazy girls would just stir yourselves a little earlier, you'd have time for a meal. I thought you were the early riser in that crowd what with sleeping outside."

Molly suffered in silence. As usual, he misunderstood her. Perhaps, she thought, they misunderstood each other always because they were sensitive and hasty, jumping into sarcastic speech without trying to fathom meanings.

As she slid off the seat at the parking lot, she made a mental resolve to go slower with Breck.

Simultaneously, he reached over to open the glove compartment and handed her a small box of raisins. "Here," he said kindly, "maybe these will help."

She tore off the cover. "Thanks. Thanks a lot."

Just as they diverged at the doors he said, "You look very pretty. Your desk will be popular this morning, though some of the male questioners may not be wholly absorbed in Yosemite."

Molly found he was right. As usual, she parried impertinent queries, "May I have the next dance?" "Tell me when the next plane leaves, please, stewardess." More than ever her airline-hostess-type cap perched on short, wavy hair inspired comments. "Are you a lady Marine?" "Well, what do you know, a Cub Scout in skirts."

Not as usual, she didn't mind such questions, though she tried to be impersonal. Unusually, she had two requests for dates and some official ranger comments. "Wow, you look great!" "Ranger Bishop, you are a decoration to the Park Service."

Compliments and good humor fed her ego, but her stomach seemed hollow. She was scheduled to give the Indian talk at ten when Gloria was due at the desk. At nine-thirty Gloria showed up.

"What are you doing here so early?" Molly asked.

"I have come to do my good deed for the day," Gloria announced, her blue eyes dancing. "I'm relieving you a half hour early so you can go feed the inner man."

"How did you know I hadn't had breakfast, Gloria?"

"A stack of beautiful, beautiful ironing outside the tent should have clued me that you hadn't had time; but I happened to answer the telephone when Breck called to talk to his wife."

"Honestly," Molly's face reddened, "all this fuss over one missed meal! Thanks, though, I'll be off."

After a quick meal, she treated herself to a new, bright lipstick to go with her hairdo. An idea for an overnight camping trip occurred to her. Maybe Foxy could accompany her.

On her lunch hour she telephoned the idea to Betty Fox; it was okayed enthusiastically. "Foxy will be thrilled, and he could be ready to leave as soon as you're through work; but aren't you forgetting one thing?"

Molly assured her, "I can pick up fresh food now; my other camping gear is always ready in my car . . . oh," she recalled, weakly, "the car! I forgot; it wouldn't run this morning."

Betty remarked, amused, "Don't worry, Breck and Irving are fiddling with it right now."

"I can fix it." Molly was instantly defensive. "I've done a lot of the work on that car myself."

"I'm sure you can," Betty replied sauvely, "but wouldn't it be easier to have it running when you come home rather than plunge in yourself and have to subtract the time from your already brief camping trip?"

"Yes." Molly frowned at the receiver. "But I don't want to ask any favors."

Betty commented tartly, "Too much independence is almost as bad as too little, my dear child. You must learn to bend a little, accept things. Independence can be a blessing or a blasphemy. Don't abuse it. See you later."

Molly hung up, smarting. Child! Here she was on the brink of her twenties, yet both of the Foxes persisted in calling her a "dear child"! Reluctantly, she admitted Gloria's accusation of immaturity to her mind as she stomped downstairs to the information desk for relief duty. At high school, college, even at camp, no one had ever labeled her anything but capable, responsible, independent, and mature.

Why, she thought rebelliously, weren't those same traits equally admirable in Yosemite? At home, she conceded, life hadn't been so compliment-strewn. There she had been criticized for being antisocial, untypical, and selfish. Like Camp 19, family life had demanded interdependent living, but at least there she had a room of her own where she could retreat.

Feet hurried by, stopped, Tim's surprised voice exclaimed, "Why, you have been hiding your light under a bushel—of hair!" He whistled admiringly, gave an exaggerated bow and asked, "How would you like to go to The Ahwahnee tonight to celebrate your emancipation? Surely, you're not shaking your head no? I may not be much, but the meals at that hotel are memorable. Do you have another date?"

"Yes, with a short, engaging youth over what may be a memorable campfire meal." Shyly she teased, warmed by his light words, backed by a serious glow in his eyes. An Ahwahnee date would have been fun, but the camping loomed more importantly.

"Who is this strange rival? Do I know him?"

"You certainly do. It is Foxy, and we are going camping."

A look of alarm replaced his amusement. "You'll be back for Monday?"

"Goodness, yes. We'll be home tomorrow night."

Later, jubilant good-byes from Foxy and sincere "Thanks for fixing my car" from Molly announced their departure.

Breck bent to close the door. "Say, where are you going? I should know."

Momentarily, she was resentful, preferring not to make plans but simply to go where whim and road dictated. Then she realized the genuine, rightful concern that was his as Foxy's father. "White Wolf," she pulled the name out of her reading. "I've never been there and I'd like to explore."

"First rate," Breck applauded, "and our naturalist there is Gordon Blake—remember the red-headed fellow at the potluck? Oh," there was a silence. "You missed that, didn't you? Well, anyway, he and his wife could probably put you up. There's usually a spare tent available." Breck's big face lit up. "I know, I'll go call him and check before you leave."

Eyes narrowed, lips tight, Molly tried not to say what she felt at his bossiness, his overbearing management of her affairs.

It was Foxy who saved the day and her temper. "Aw, Dad, we want to camp by ourselves! Staying with the Blakes would be just like Camp 19."

Betty echoed, "He's right, dear, let them go. They want to be independent, not tied down to anyone."

Molly flashed her a grateful look and was even more grateful she had held her tongue when Breck said, "Of course, of course, I didn't mean to interfere. Have fun, take pictures, and don't sleep with any bear."

Molly recalled his jovial warning when she woke to a clanging noise before dawn. A squint at the sky showed stars paling out in a slate-colored sky. Another clang suggested a bear raiding the garbage can. Nothing to worry about. Their campsite, the farthest one back, was yards away from trash can, faucet, or camper's tent. She rolled over to check on Foxy, but could see only a hump in the bag that had left the air mattress for tarp-covered ground.

Smiling sleepily, she pulled her bag up around cold ears and closed her eyes. A ripping sound jerked her awake and out of bed. Reflecting quickly that brother-bruin must be tearing a camper's tent, she yanked on jeans, sweat shirt, and shoes, grabbed a flashlight in one hand, rocks in the other, and raced off.

A scream split the air as the bear tore canvas. Molly saw him, big and black, standing on his hind feet, scenting food. Her first rock hit him in the chest.

"Make some noise," Molly called toward the tent inhabitants. Knowing a bear feared noise and light, she yelled *"Hoocha, hoocha"* and pegged more stones. They didn't hurt the startled bear, but annoyed him.

He gave a "whoof," dropped to all fours, and started toward her.

Molly didn't panic, remembering that bear have very poor eyesight so he probably was running blindly. From the tent someone began whacking pans together noisily; and just as she was ready to run herself, a pair of headlights shot on and a horn honked.

All the clamor was too much for the bear, who swerved away from Molly and crashed off toward the river.

"Wow," Molly muttered, exhilarated, eyes wide with excitement. People were running up; voices called, "Is he gone?" and she was proud to tell them, "Everything's all right. No casualties except the garbage can."

Eyes enormous in her flashbeam, Foxy asked tremulously, "Shall I turn off the car lights?"

"Was that you? Smart boy!" She hugged him hard, then commanded, "Climb back in bed before you freeze, while I go check on the campers."

Kneeling at the tent door, she confronted several pairs of frightened eyes. A man, his wife, and three children regarded her in the illuminated upheaval of sleeping bags, pans, blankets, food, fresh cantaloupes, and clothes. "He's long gone," she reassured them, "and I don't think he'll come back for more."

"Let's leave," the woman said glassily.

Patiently, Molly told her of bear habits, their disinterest in people, their passion for food. Eventually, the man boomed heartily, "It's almost daylight now; guess I'll do a little fishing. You all right, honey?"

Molly withdrew to the coziness of her sleeping bag, but sleep was as far away as the moon. Excitement kept her tense and wide-eyed while the mountain world awoke. Long before anyone but fishermen were about, squirrels, chipmunks, birds, and marmots were active.

She woke Foxy; and as they prepared breakfast,

the bear-scared man brought them a string of fresh-caught trout.

"Don't thank me," he protested. "It's the other way around, believe me. Not only do I thank you for chasing the bear off, but also for calming us so that our camping trip didn't end with an anti-mountain family."

Molly cautioned, "The only times you should be really leery of a bear is when a cub is around too, or when a bear is actually in your food. That's no time to try to scare one away."

After that, she and Foxy spent a delightful day apart from people. Their wanderings took them far down the river over granite, around pools, through aspen and lodgepole, and around still-swampy meadows. Foxy fished while she photographed wild flowers—lovely shooting stars and tufted Indian paintbrush. Both recaptured sleep on a sandy flat beside the river. By the time they hiked back into camp, people were trooping toward a campfire circle; and the sky was washed with dusk.

"Hey, here's a note from Ranger Blake on our table." Foxy picked up his discovery and read it to Molly. *"Plan to have dinner with us between 6:30 and 7:30, then attend campfire if you'd like. Truly looking forward to meeting you!"*

A little crossly, Molly declared, "Your father must have called him after all. Anyway, it's far too late to go. Let's have dinner and leave so we'll be at Camp 19 before your dad calls out the bloodhounds."

Foxy said disconsolately, "I wish he hadn't done that—just when you were starting to like him."

Silently, she agreed.

CHAPTER VII

Her irritation with Breck was multiplied when, after their arrival, he dragged her into the tent. "I insist you have a cup of cof—whoops, I mean cocoa—and tell us your adventures. Did you see the Blakes?"

"No, it was eight o'clock, campfire time, before we staggered into camp." Half-angrily she added, "After you called, he left us a note asking us for dinner."

Breck's generous lower lip dropped. "After I called! Oh, no, Molly, I didn't, nor would I have when you both said you wanted to be on your own! No, he telephoned me to find out more about you."

"Why?" she demanded prickily, already tired from the day, the talk, the lone, dazzling light bulb, and the people-surrounded feeling she hated. "Our camp was neat, and I checked twice to be sure our fire was out."

"Down, girl, down." Betty Fox's eyes twinkled as she passed cookies.

"My," Breck soothed, "you are the touchy one."

Suddenly, Foxy blurted, "I bet I know why Ranger Blake phoned—to tell about that dumb bear Molly scared away."

"You helped!" Molly corrected, affectionately reaching over to tousle his hair. "Here's the smart guy who thought to blow the horn and turn on the headlights."

"Good for you, Son," Breck beamed. "I'm proud of you both. You see, Blake had a report from those grateful campers, and by reading your automobile registration found your name. Of course, he had heard of your being on the staff so he called to verify. I didn't know about the dinner invitation, but he wanted to meet you. Am I forgiven for supposed interference?" His eyes met hers.

"Certainly," she muttered, embarrassed at this newest misunderstanding. "I didn't even leave a note at his tent to explain about our not accepting. Guess I should have."

Betty agreed, "I should say so! However, I'll take you off the hook this time by telephoning White Wolf."

Molly stood, stifled a yawn, and dug in her pockets. "I brought you a couple of rocks, and I did take several flower pictures. And now, please excuse me, but I need a shower and sleep."

"Naturaly, naturally, you're excused—this time!"

A note in the tent blotted her almost perfect day. Brisk printing marched across binder paper, and engaging animal cartoons decorated the margins and negative words.

A pictured doe seemed to be saying: *"Dear Molly: Forgive Muir-tracked-mind me, but one of his descendants is in the Valley just for today and tomorrow; and, inevitably, I am being chauffeur, guide, listener, and interviewer. Tim says postponing our Coulterville Road exploration a week is all right. How about you?"*

A bear figure asked, *"Bearable?"*

A postscript added, *"Perhaps our raincheck day will be as Muir describes, '. . . when the first level sunbeams sting the domes and spires, with what a burst of power the big, wild days begin!' "*

At first, Molly read the unique note with a welling of disappointment and dismay. Had she known its contents sooner, she and Foxy could have enjoyed White Wolf another day. Re-reading Dutch's words, she was bolstered by their individuality, the soulful sketches, and the Muir quote. Carefuly, she put it in her own filling naturalist notebook; then took her weary self to bed.

She woke not to morning and dawn light, but to lightning flashes showing wind-tossed trees, and wonderful, sonorous, echoing thunder. Storms had fascinated her since childhood; a Yosemite storm would be a new experience. She knew its dangers—lightning strikes bred flames, wind might fan them; but rain would lay the dust, refresh the mountain world and swell streams.

Quickly she covered her bedroll with a tarp, leaving only her expectant face exposed. Large, warm raindrops began to splatter. She thought of the thousands of campers who would be tearing around covering things, doubling families up in tents and cars, rather than enjoying the good smell of dampened dirt.

A floppy rain hat protected her head as drops spattered onto her face. She licked her lips and opened her mouth for more, enjoying the taste and the feel as the rain quickened, hardened. Thunder quieted as rain beat down upon leaf, bush, rock, ground, and tree.

"Molly? Where the devil are you?" Breck's annoyed voice called, and a strong light darted about. It lit her face. "Don't just lie there," he commanded. "Come on, quick; I'll help you move into our tent."

"I don't want to leave." Wind grabbed her yelled words. "I'm enjoying it."

"Enjoying?" he trumpeted incredulously, looming over her in bulky, dripping raincoat. "Are you crazy? You'll be soaked and catch your death of cold."

Still immobile, she answered his anger. "No, I won't. Except for my face, I'm covered and warm. See?"

"I think you are out of your mind." His voice shook with anger. "Believe me, this is the last time I ever try to help you!"

She watched him stalk off, then heard him bellow, "Stay there, Laura. She doesn't want help. She just wants to be alone to *enjoy* the storm! Go back to bed. One of us getting soaked for nothing is enough."

Molly's eyes narrowed and her mind answered him, "Nobody asked you to leave your warm bed! If I wanted shelter, I'm perfectly capable of carrying my sleeping bag to the tent."

After that encounter, the storm seemed less exhilarating, though lightning still cracked open the sky and the rainfall became more savage. Her face was numb, her eyes smarting, before she pulled the tarp over her head and turned on her stomach for sleep. It did not come. But noise on the tarp did. Airlessness caused her to lift up the tarp with one hand, letting in damp air.

Unbidden thoughts came in too. Breck's interference had been kindly meant, stirred by a fatherly concern. She was glad her resentment hadn't found speech; he had been infuriated enough by not comprehending her real enjoyment. That was over. Now she felt hot, uncomfortable, and trapped. If she gave in and ran for the tent, Breck would say "I told you so." This idea kept her a few more minutes, during which the rain showed no signs of slackening. Then she thought, "So what?"

Between pulling herself out of bed, scooping bag, tarp, and mattress into her arms, and staggering toward the tent, she was thoroughly soaked. Surprisingly, a light lit her way, and the front door opened magically as she half fell up the steps.

"Thank goodness you came in." Laura helped her place her bedroll on the extra cot. "I've been stewing like an old mother hen."

"Well, cluck somewhere else," Molly retorted. "I'm fine. I don't need any help."

Laura's cold-creamed face sagged, and colored in reaction.

Molly's impulsive words echoed in her ears as she glanced about. A teakettle steamed on the wood stove whose heat she drew near; her other pajamas and a big turkish towel hung over a chair; the light, the opened door—all illustrated Laura's concern.

Molly grabbed Laura's arm. "Forgive me for being mulish again." She shivered convulsively. "I guess I do need help. Thanks for everything."

Slowly, the older woman's expression lost its stiffness. "You need dry clothes and a cup of hot tea." She ignored both rebuke and plea. "Towel yourself dry and climb into your pajamas."

Molly complied, drying herself vigorously before downing the warming tea. Another glance showed her an open book. That had kept Laura occupied while she had waited for Molly. A wave of appreciation made her feel touched.

"What are you reading?"

"Better wash your cold, dirty feet in this." Laura shoved a basin of stove-heated water toward her. "Why, a book of John Muir's in which he tells about the ecstasy of a storm."

"Was he out in it?"

"I should say so, in a far more exposed position than yours. He was riding a treetop, exulting in the full feel of rain and wind." Laura paused, brow knit. "From his words, I shared your experience vicariously, but," she added honestly, "I was glad when you came in."

Molly wiggled her toes in the warm water, sipped her tea, and listened to rain assaulting the canvas tent. "Me too. Thanks for mothering me."

Was maturity synonymous with conformity? Was her valued independence nothing but nonconformity? Certainly, she had acted with maturity by coming in and accepting Laura's fussy kindness. Honesty made her admit that the storm had forced her in, and that, at first, she had rebuffed Laura as, earlier, she had sent Breck away seething.

Such disturbing thoughts kept her awake until she determined to give more of herself, enter into camp doings, maybe even attend one of the nightly get togethers.

Between soul-searching, the rain, the strange bed, and being inside, Molly slept fitfully and was up early and excitedly to see drifting fog. By the time she was dressed and out, even the drizzle had ceased; and all the world and its noises seemed wrapped in cotton.

At times as she walked, a solid wall of fog would move, inexorably, toward her; other times half the Valley appeared gray and spiderwebby. Once, her sense of direction was affected so that she wandered pathlessly.

Abruptly, she bumped into something solid that emitted a bear-like "Ooff."

Fog swirled upward, revealing a uniformed ranger who said, politely, "Excuse me, ma'm."

The voice alerted Molly. "Dutch! Isn't this wonderful?"

He moved closer, staring. "Yes. Is that you, Molly girl, under all those layers of clothes?"

Dutch explained that he was on his way to The Ahwahnee for breakfast with the Muir relative, and wasn't it a good thing they had postponed the trip since driving in such a fog would be dangerous? She agreed, and said she was loving the Valley's being so secret and mysterious. He walked into the swallowing fog.

She thrust her hands in her pockets; and though her feet trod carefully, her heart took giant steps as she re-heard the tenderness in his tone saying, "Molly girl."

Most of the morning, she bent over books and a file of Yosemite magazines, reading about Muir, Galen Clark, and everything she could find by Amos Vanderbunt.

Eventually, gorged with words, ideas, and the library warmth, she wandered back to camp. Sun had blazed away the fog's density, but the day was still cool and pleasant.

Irving's wife, Marcy, stamped out of the telephone booth as Molly sauntered by. "Trouble?" she asked.

"The baby sitter can't come, and I have an appointment to have my hair cut before Irving's folks come this weekend."

"Too bad," Molly murmured and passed on, insulated against such trivia. As she started to spread a sandwich, she thought again of Marcy's face—tired, disappointed—her hair hanging lankly to her shoulders. Remembering what her own haircut had done, she rushed over to Marcy's tent, offering, "I'll baby sit."

"You will? Are you sure? The boys are no trouble, but the baby has to be fed and changed."

"Do I look helpless?" Molly demanded.

"No, it's just that you're always so busy with outdoor projects; it's hard to conceive of you changing diapers or being domestic."

"Try me." Molly wondered if she seemed that selfish and alien to all the camp women.

While the baby slept and the boys played, she ironed the rest of Gloria's dresses, and observed camp doings with interest. Someone was at, coming, or going to the washing machine almost constantly. Pine needles flew as children played energetically. Jays squawked as brooms swept tent stoops. One mother herded a troup of the older youngsters off to swim in the river; another sang.

Later, several women drifted in front of the Fox tent to perch, chattering, on straight chairs and a stump. Molly snorted to herself, foolish, aimless, women talk.

After Grace, the baby, woke, was dressed and fed, she

toddled outdoors. Molly followed at a distance. Grace waddled to Betty Fox who called casually, "Join us?"

There was little else she could do, though she dreaded teasing about her role and women talk. Surprisingly, the animated talk was of hikes.

Betty said positively, "I think climbing Half Dome's the most rewarding climb."

"Wait till you try Mt. Dana. Now there's a real hike."

"Yes, the views are incredible."

Another woman put in enthusiastically, "So are the ones from Glacier Point, and that Four Mile Trail's no slouch."

"Too public," Betty objected. "I like a hike where you can be alone with nature part of the time instead of constantly meeting other hikers."

"What's your favorite hike?" Rowena Johnson turned to Molly, who was all ears.

"I haven't taken many yet," she confessed. "The Vernal and Nevada Falls trail is my least favorite—as Betty says, it's too public. My first day off I hiked to the top of El Capitan from Tamarack Flat. That was lovely. The trail's overgrown, the views are glorious, and the wilderness belongs to you."

"Sounds perfect," Rowena said. "I'd like to try."

Their talk veered slightly to the practicability of various packs and baby carriers. Molly appreciated their achievements more as she envisioned them encumbered with papoose carriers, tagging children, and attendant problems.

Marcy arrived back, pretty and neat. "Stay for dinner," she invited lightly. "I already have asked Tim."

"I can't." Molly's answer was automatic and blunt.

"Why not? It's your day off."

Molly hesitated, searching for a reason for her negativism. Perhaps she was so used to refusing camp overtures, she didn't know how to say yes.

"Stay," one of the boys begged.

"All right, I will, thanks; but let me go home first and clean up."

There she hung Gloria's clothes, replaced her sleeping bag, and cut a big stack of kindling. A glimpse of Laura awkwardly handling a hatchet that morning had shown Molly how she could repay her for unexpected kindness. A hatchet should fit into a hand naturally, she thought, amused, not be wielded as a battering ram.

Thinking of Tim, she dressed with care, applied lipstick before a mirror, and twice knotted Laura's scarf around her neck in an attempt for a casual look.

Her reward came with wolf whistles from Foxy and Tim and a blunt, "You don't look much like a drowned rat now," from Breck.

Good-naturedly she parried, "You should have seen me when I gave up and swam in."

"Oh, you came to your senses, did you?"

She clamped her lips and joined Tim, muttering, "Whenever he opens his mouth, he puts my foot in it."

Tim's sparkling, approving eyes erased any annoyance from her mind. "Let's take all our feet and go dancing later, shall we?"

His attentiveness and Dutch's "Molly girl" were new, strangely appealing attentions to Molly, whose abrupt manners and aloofness had kept boys at arm's length.

The following afternoon she was slated for two hours of desk duty, and reluctantly left the sunny outdoors for the museum's cool gloom. Irving limped in.

"Sorry if I'm the ninetieth person to ask, but why are you hobbling?" Molly asked.

Irving scowled. "Twisted my ankle leading a nature walk this morning. And right now, I'm slated for contact duty in Camp 15."

Molly knew that contact duty was a program designed to give campers a chance to talk to and question a naturalist. Although she had never done it, she surmised that it would be more enjoyable than what she was doing.

"I'll trade you jobs," she offered eagerly. "You take the desk; I'll take the camp."

"Fine with me, but Breck may not like it. His schedules never seem to slate you for contact work."

"Don't worry, he won't care," Molly assured him.

While she was putting her bike in the racks at Camp 15, a teen-ager cracked, "I thought all rangers drove patrol cars or rode horseback. Why are you different?"

"I'm a ranger-naturalist," she replied quickly, "and a naturalist likes to walk to observe nature firsthand."

"Ha," a man commented, "all you can observe around here is human nature, and some of it's ugly."

Challenged by his sourness, she looked around intently. Obviously he saw only tents, washing draped on lines, cars, children racing about, and people in every state of dress and undress, humor, and temper. A crowded campground subtracted from a woods adventure.

"Try to look around with a naturalist's eyes," she advised, nervously aware that she was attracting an audience. "By the faucet here is a raccoon's pawprint. See? Behind you is a wonderful old black oak whose gnarled branches support bird and squirrel nests.

"Those darting grosbeaks may be a nuisance, but think of the hordes of mosquitoes they eat daily. On this fine cedar tree you can see the holes made by woodpeckers. Some of them may be the homes of bats."

"Stop!" the man exclaimed in mock dismay, "I'm convinced. From now on, I'll develop a naturalist eye."

Children tagged her as she strolled through camp, often pausing to answer questions. Seemingly, 80 percent of all queries concerned bear; either campers complaining that they hadn't seen one, or complaining that they had.

A girl volunteered, "A boy has a squirrel in a cage over by the meadow."

"Are you sure? Show me." Keeping wild animals captive was one of Molly's real hates.

Near a tent that fronted on a grassy swale, a sullen teen-ager cradled a box. "Stool pigeon," he glared at the girl; then turning to Molly, he said belligerently, "I suppose you want my squirrel."

She firmly stated. "I want to see it."

Defensively, the boy showed her. "It's in a big box with mosquito netting for a cover. See, I give it water and food."

Spurned water and cookie crumbs lay beside a beautiful gray squirrel whose bushy, fluffy tail took up most of the box. Its bright, beady eyes looked up fearfully.

"He needs acorns and pine seeds," Molly said hotly, "not chocolate chip cookies." Again she checked anger.

"What good is he doing you caged? Wouldn't it be more fun to watch him scamper up a tree with that tail fanning out?"

"I was going to let him go this evening anyway." The boy yanked off the netting, and the squirrel was gone in one graceful bound. "I suppose you'll arrest me now."

Offhand, she couldn't recall what the rule was on trapping squirrels. Thoughtfully, she studied the scowling boy, whose chin and lower lip jutted out. His black eyes smouldered resentfully.

"What's your name and how old are you?"

"Darrel Black. I'm fifteen. So what?"

Instead of telling him the precepts of a national park that allowed every animal freedom and preservation from man, she said firmly, "I want you to show up for Junior Rangers the rest of the mornings you stay in the Valley. You're too old to participate in the program, but we need a strong arm."

"Okay." His tone was indifferent, but his eyes flickered with interest.

She pressed her advantage. "I want you to read the mammal pamphlet, then list the different kinds of squirrels, and where they might be found in the Park. You can turn that report in to me at 8:45 tomorrow morning at the Happy Isles Nature Center. See you there."

She walked off before he could refuse or challenge her, hoping that she had used the authority of her uniform wisely.

"Hey, Ranger . . ." a camper called her back to the job she liked best—interpreting nature.

CHAPTER VIII

"Since when do you do the scheduling?" inquired Breck when he saw Molly in camp that evening.

She colored. "I simply traded duty with Irving because of his ankle. I was sure you wouldn't mind."

"Well, I do mind your not checking with me first, and I mind your wandering through any public campground alone."

Molly sighed, "Here we go again! But, Breck, I was rarely alone. Most of the time children, some of them Junior Rangers, chaperoned me, and people kept gathering to ask questions. It was fun; I wish you would schedule me for that often."

"I won't," he exploded angrily. "You seem to forget my responsibility to you."

"Your *what?*" Her body stiffened. "I don't need any privileges or care."

"You do if any of the two-legged wolves in camps start bothering you. That's what I'm thinking about."

"That's ridiculous," she stomped off and fumed to Gloria, who was painstakingly polishing her fingernails in the tent.

After her angry recital, Gloria advised, "Calm down, my ruffled friend. As usual you two clashed and said hasty things you didn't mean. You know how touchy Breck is; if you'd asked him about exchanging duty, he would have approved it. Then, instead of apologizing, you waved a red flag and told him you loved the job and wanted to do it again.

"Being Breck, he reacted negatively and gave you the first objection that came into his head. Don't look so thunderous. He's just being fatherly."

Violently, Molly exclaimed, "One father's enough. I left him at home so I could be free and independent."

"There you go again," Gloria commented. "You would have made an ideal woman suffragette. Molly B. Anthony. Don't glare at me so, you'll shrivel my nail polish."

Molly queried sulkily, "Am I being immature?"

"Yes." Gloria smiled at her shrewdly and kindly. "Bristlingly independent too, but you are improving. You're not nearly so self-centered."

"Thanks for nothing," Molly muttered, and left the tent, not to run away for a perspective-returning walk, but to the bear baffle for food which she had bought after work.

After thumping meat and salad makings down on the table, she looked threateningly at Gloria. "Don't you dare say one word. I bought steaks for all of us to thank you for friendship." The sincere, though infuriated,

110

words tore out of her, leaving her breathless and crimson.

Gloria's pretty composure crumpled into lines of merriment and laughter. Momentarily, Molly bridled; then, tantalized, laughed tentatively.

"So did I," Gloria chortled, explaining, "I bought fillets to thank you for the ironing, and Laura for patience with her messy roommate."

Darrel Black was waiting for Molly by the rail fence when she bicycled in the next morning.

"Here's my homework." A half-grin took the sarcasm from his words as he handed her a piece of paper. "Now what do I do?"

"Help me carry the snake cases over from the building, please."

Before they were through with the job, she had a dismaying thought. Breck wouldn't like her moving the snakes, a man's job, with a strange helper. Why hadn't she told him about Darrel, about her trial at teaching rather than punishing him? It would be just like Breck to charge in, rightfully, she admitted, and undo what little good she might be doing Darrel. Her hastily conceived idea seemed feeble in the truly cold light of morning. Passing color books and crayons out would not be Darrel's idea of boy's work.

When she saw Breck drive in, she hurried over. Predictably, he growled, "Who's that?"

"Darrel Black. Please don't lose your temper, Breck, but I need help with him. It's a long story, but he's here to help as sort of a punishment for catching a squirrel."

111

Breck's expression was foreboding enough so that she continued frantically, "Please help, Breck. I should have explained last night, but I think it's important to change his philosophy."

"All right." His scowl was unrelenting. "Carry these papers over so our concern over him won't be so obvious."

"Our concern. . . ." The words warmed her as she obeyed.

Shortly, Darrel was carrying wood for a campfire; later she heard sounds of chopping and half-heard Breck telling him what kinds of feed to gather for the snakes.

While she was relieved not to be responsible for him, it annoyed her slightly that Breck had converted the boy so quickly. Darrel even talked like a naturalist, explaining to the Chipmunk group, "All these snakes will be released this fall. They are kept just so people can observe them and learn why snakes are important."

Handling snakes always brought stifled shrieks from little girls and quieter, though respectful, reactions from the boys. Molly led the Deer group of ten- and eleven-year-olds on the nature walk that day. At a pool in the meadow she caught a water snake and asked casually, "What good do you suppose this fellow does?"

"Eats fish," a boy volunteered.

Carefully, she let the reptile back in the water where it glided gracefully away. "Do you think he swims fast enough to catch a smart fish?"

A chorus of "No's" reached her. Molly looked at their reflected images in the shallow pool. Grass brushed their knees, faces were puzzled, wrinkled with thinking, or awed; not one was indifferent. What a wonderful place to be, she thought, loving the blue and gold and green world, her job and her charges.

A girl guessed, "Maybe that snake catches sick fish so the river doesn't get full of them."

"Right," Molly beamed. "A reptile like that is valuable for a control in nature."

"Is even a rattlesnake good for something?" Enormous awe sounded in a pig-tailed girl's question.

Molly knelt, smoothed grass, and exposed a hole. "What do you suppose lives here?"

"A gopher?" "Rats?" "Ground squirrels?"

Molly explained, "Rats, mice, and ground squirrels carry diseases. Rattlesnakes keep their population down to a safe number. Do any of you live on farms?"

"I do, I do, and I betcha I know what you're going to say." The farmer's son was big with importance. "Gopher snakes are the farmer's friend, more than rattlers. A gopher chews young roots and destroys berry bushes, but the good old gopher snake gobbles them up by sliding into holes like this one."

Back at the work tables, she let them examine a beautifully marked mountain king snake who somehow slid off the table and started moving fluidly for the tall grass. A great shriek went up, and Molly ran to recapture the snake. Darrel flashed by, grasped the runaway, and returned it to her.

"I'm glad you're here," she said, truthfully.

"Me too," he grinned. "Maybe I'll be a ranger someday."

Breck interrupted, "There are different kinds of

rangers. In the National Park Service we have two kinds —protective rangers who patrol, fight fire, and try to preserve nature; and ranger-naturalists, like us, who study and interpret nature to alert people to the reasons behind preservation and conservation."

Darrel straightened proudly. "That's the kind I want to be, a ranger-naturalist."

After all that amiability, Molly was unready for Breck's sternness after everyone had gone. "Your idea of converting Darrel, rather than antagonizing him by punishment, worked out well."

"Thanks to your taking over," she put in hastily.

"Yes. After this, don't take authority in your own hands without consulting someone higher up. You acted unwisely." Graveness was etched in his face as he looked at her steadily. "You say you want contact duty again, and yet you acted impulsively without any stated authority while on your first campground tour."

"And last?" she asked bitterly.

"Possibly, though I believe in giving people second chances. I'm sorry to have friction between us again, my dear."

"Don't call me that," she flashed, goaded beyond courtesy at his unendearing term of address. Until then she had gritted mental teeth whenever he used it; now, suddenly, it was unbearable, piled as it was on top of constant disapproval and even earned, official rebuke. "I am not your 'dear' or anyone else's."

A hurt look, quickly veiled in somber anger, crossed his face. Curtly, he agreed, "You certainly aren't! It must be wonderful to be so independent, so lofty of others.

One more thing. I put you on schedule for a campfire talk tomorrow night."

Keeping her expression blank, she stared at him with flashing eyes. How unfair, how cruel to give her only a day and a half's warning. There would be little off-duty time to prepare a talk, and he knew her dread of crowds. This must be his way of paying her back.

"What is my announced subject?"

Her cold sarcasm reached him for he answered, "Ah, Molly, Indians of Yosemite, of course. Isn't that your specialty? You have made your preference so plain, so often."

She looked away, remembering her taking over at the Indian program, her arrowhead-making demonstration which had appeared show-offy to him. "Indians will be fine. May I leave now?"

"Molly, why must you bring out the worst in me? I am not your enemy. . . ."

Unfeelingly, she repeated, "May I leave?"

His momentarily vulnerable face tightened, creased in forbidding lines. "Yes, please do."

After dinner that evening, Molly surrounded herself with books and articles on Indians. A fresh tablet of paper, a stack of index cards, and two sharp pencils awaited use.

Compassionately, Laura withdrew. "I'm going to the movie. Good luck, my dear."

Molly nodded, appreciating the "my dear" as heartfelt from her new friend.

Less understandingly, Gloria tousled Molly's hair as

she left, trailing perfume, for a date. "You'll do all right if you omit two thirds of the facts you find in those books. And, Molly, I think you are misunderstanding Breck again. I think he knew the agony of preparation you would plunge into and gave you a short time deliberately to spare you."

"Deliberately, yes. Spare me, no. He should have given me a week. I need it for a proper talk."

"Thank goodness, you don't have it." Gloria let the screendoor slam after her. "Laura and I couldn't stand a whole week of your being tortured."

Molly read intently, made notes, started an outline, and tried hard not to think of the mass of people who would be listening to her.

A knock sounded. She glanced up and out to see Dutch silhouetted against the darkening sky.

"Care to join me for a walk?" he asked formally.

"Oh, Dutch, I can't!" She motioned to the jumbled material on the table. "I'm up to my ears in studying for my campfire talk tomorrow."

He didn't argue, saying only, "Come anyway. There'll be a moon."

His quietness heightened her excuses. "This is torture. How can I pack the entire history, tradition, and living conditions of Yosemite Indians in one half-hour talk? I must read, absorb material, organize. . . ." She interrupted her frantic words. "Didn't Muir have something reassuring to say for stress?"

"Almost everything he wrote, said, or did urged going into the wilderness for beauty, rest and peace." Dutch turned away.

116

"He was right." Abruptly, she unwound from the bench, yanked off the single pull light and strode to the door. "Wait. I'm coming with you."

"Because of Muir or me?"

"You." Her answer was shy.

Their first aimless stop was under an overhead light by Sentinel Bridge. Dutch indicated the road to the west edged by giant locust trees, cedars, oaks, and to the left, dimly seen, hulking, granite boulders. "Old Village," he began softly, animation livening his lean, tanned face, "the scene of pioneer Yosemite activity. Somehow, the Sentinel Hotel crowded here between the dusty stagecoach road and the river. In the summer guests swam in the Merced; in the winter blocks of ice were cut and stored in sawdust-lined icehouses."

As they walked slowly down the road, he continued, "To our right stood hotel buildings; to our left more buildings, tents, the blacksmith shop, a carpenter shop, the Wells Fargo office."

Thanks to Dutch, the deserted, grass-grown scene came alive with the squeak of buggy wheels, the whap of whips, the thudding of many heels on boardwalk. Residents, tourists, and Indians had jammed the store. . . .

". . . for food, calico, buttons, haircuts, medicines, ice cream, gossip, news—the substance and breath of life."

"Even then there were too many people," she commented. "How did Muir feel?"

Dutch chuckled, "Like you, he was alternately appalled and inspired. Appalled because human erosion was causing overcivilization, a wilderness herd; inspired

117

because the people recognized uniqueness and helped form Yosemite as a national sanctuary. Muir had to have their help before fostering the conservation idea to President Theodore Roosevelt."

They stopped often in quiet awe, seeing the Valley like a white lake in the moonlight, seeing Yosemite Falls a carved column of alabaster. Treetops were etched sharply. The sky was flooded with brightness. Every cliff was magical, white in contrast to black shadows.

Molly had no adjectives, no admiring words, only a heart full of awe at such beauty. Gently, she promoted, "Muir said. . . ."

Dutch smiled down at her, eyes luminous under whitish brows that raised wrinkles toward his rough, wheat-colored hair. "Don't you care what Vanderbunt says?"

Her ears took in the teasing tone, but her eyes showed her the intentness, the caring in firm lines at the corners of his suddenly tightened mouth. "Yes, I do care, Dutch. I barely know the you beneath the Muir student."

"And you want to?" He led her to a meadow-sitting log.

"Yes." Her unquiet heart asked, Were you a sober little boy? Did beauty make tears burn your eyes? Were you ever afraid of anything? What do you want of life?

There was no levity to him as he spoke. "Mountains have been my life since my childhood on a Sierra ranch. I knew beauty early. Sunrises hurt with their vast brilliance, their colored promises. I knew pain early too. My father was killed in a horse accident when I was eleven. My mother became embittered, took me away to Oakland where I found a different beauty; but I longed always for a mountain to look at. A boy needs a mountain to inspire him."

Frogs garrumped in the silence as his speech ceased. His story pained Molly.

"Did you need a mountain too?" he asked incisively.

"Yes, and I had one, a whole range of them, from the Monday after school let out until the Friday after Labor Day. My parents sent me to summer camp year after year, and I lived for it during the nine, long city months."

"Do you hate cities so?"

"I do, and I disliked regimentation at camp, but there were times alone and interests and always the heart-holding mountains to see, explore, and sustain me." Molly was breathless. Never had she spoken so deeply, feelingly before. It was as if another self dredged the words up from memory, experience, maturity.

Abashed, she directed him back to his childhood. "You escaped to the mountains from Oakland?"

"Not escaped," his eyes were merry in the moon-light. "That's the wrong word because I have room in my heart for Oakland and San Francisco, for fog and city streets at night, but the Sierra is my passion. There was no money to send me to camp; but I was strong and fairly capable so I worked summers after I was fourteen, on a cattle ranch neighboring the one owned by my dad."

"Is it still yours?" His voice had shown love.

"Sixty acres are mine still," his tone showed triumph and pride, then sadness; "the other sixty acres were sold to bury my mother, and help put me through college."

She pictured him resolute, angular, independent. "When did Yosemite come in?"

"When I was five on my first camping trip with my dad. Virginia Canyon, my first trout. . . ."

She saw a thin, determined boy clutching a bent fishing rod fiercely. A huge, triumphant grin swallowing freckles. "Dad, look, *look!*"

Dutch talked on. "But Yosemite began to dominate my life the day I took the job as summer museum aid. That was the summer I discovered John Muir and beauty, stopped hurting and began living."

"Why did you become a teacher then instead of a Ranger-naturalist?"

"Because through Muir I discovered California history and literature. After graduating to a summer naturalist, I discovered I could interpret *and* teach. I don't mean to brag."

Modesty rendered his face vulnerable. She was shaken. He was not wholly independent; he cared what others thought, what she thought! She longed to touch him, express her pride in his accomplishments, show her caring. Instead, she hated the prim, proper words that eased from her lips. "You have something to brag about. Your lectures are fine, valuable."

"Thanks." He was noncommittal, abruptly reserved.

She wondered if he were regretting his telling, his sharing his life with her. "Dutch," she said urgently, "I read everything I could find that you've written on Yosemite. Everything from the birds you observed as a museum aid to recent essays on Muir. You're good,

Dutch, searching and sensitive; and you have changed from a naturalist to a historian."

"You saw that?" he marveled aloud. "You went to the trouble of reading all my youthful stuff, and could see the change?"

"Yes. What does it mean?"

"Beyond the biography of Muir, I can't predict, but it means more studying, more teaching, more living, and more Yosemite."

Abruptly, he changed the subject. "How old are you?"

"Twenty." In a few days, she added to herself.

He cupped her chin in his hard, right palm, saying almost to himself. "Twenty! You have old thoughts for such a young head."

You're only twenty-four, she wanted to argue, but held silent. Four years older than herself. Still, after hearing of his life, she realized that those four years signified experience, pain, and maturity far beyond her. Briefly, she regretted that her life had been so smooth and depth-free; then she shook the thought away, realizing how lucky she was to have two living parents, a sister, and an income that made physical independence feasible.

How shallow her existence must seem to Dutch, who had struggled for his. How young she must seem. She sighed.

"Come on, Molly girl, let's go home."

Dutch walked beside her, head up and hands deep in his pockets. She wished he would hold her hand as Tim had, but the affectionate "Molly girl" had been almost as tangible.

After Junior Rangers the next day, Molly had a two hour break. Like a squirrel darting for a hole, she headed for the museum training room. Laura helped pile her desk high with the same material on Indians she had fled the night before. Other rangers were studying or writing at their desks, but the room was quiet except for the noisy, air-cooling fan.

Intently, she began to outline subjects to cover—history, food, shelter, clothing, weapons, and customs. Balls of wadded paper tumbled onto the floor. After nervously chewing off her lipstick, she chewed on a pencil. Her watch read 1:23; her talk was scheduled for eight-thirty and from two until six she was on schedule. That left thirty-seven minutes now and approximately two hours that evening to prepare her talk. The outline was dull; she ripped it up.

A hearty voice startled her. "Well, well, a little stage fright?"

Resentfully, she looked up at Breck.

"Why, I didn't think you were afraid of anything. Don't tell me an audience of campers scares you?"

Conscious of the other rangers' attention, she nodded numbly, feeling tormented and hating her tormentor.

Breck ceased his peculiar humor to advise, kindly, "Take my advice and throw away your notes. Just talk naturally as you have done so well at other Indian programs. Have you picked your slides?"

"Not yet." It dumbfounded her that he could be helpful after being so harsh. Evidently they were to start fresh with each other again. Maybe, she thought grimly, he bore no grudges, but she did.

"You haven't? Well, my de—," he coughed and then began anew, "Well, Molly, go in, choose your slides, put them in subject order, and then outline your remarks from them. Stop looking so stricken. You've talked on Indians a dozen times without any illustrations to help. With slides, talking will be much easier."

"Thanks," she said sincerely, erasing grudges from her memory. It occurred to her that Gloria might be right in that Breck had deliberately given her scant time to stew over her talk. In the next half hour she selected color slides from the reservoir of those taken by naturalists over the years.

"Thought I'd find you here." Tim poked his smiling face in. "Dutch and I have a few new slides you might want to use. There's one of Julia Parker weaving baskets, and one of you I took when you weren't looking."

"Me? Doing what?"

"Showing Camp 19 children how to make arrowheads. If you talk about that, it would make a good illustration."

"Thanks, Tim." She was touched by his concern.

"Don't thank me," he teased, "I'm master of ceremonies tonight, and I'm just making sure you have a good program. I'll buy you a cup of coffee afterward."

"I hope you won't be disappointed." She wished Dutch had given the offhand invitation; but he, she knew from checking the schedule, was leading an all-day hike.

CHAPTER IX

At the Camp 7 amphitheater that night, Tim led group singing. It was loud, enthusiastic, sometimes even harmonious. Molly walked around, adding wood to the campfire, answering some questions, and spotting faces she knew in the audience.

Half the Junior Rangers seemed to be sitting in front vigorously supplying motions for "Ichbin der Conductor." Darrel Black waved at her from back; Laura was plunked in front, her eyes betraying compassionate interest.

So, Molly thought, I have a friendly audience, and once Tim finishes, a relaxed one as well. My slides are good, all in order so that a click of my finger will flash them on the screen. There's nothing to worry about. Nothing. Then why did her skin pull tight across her face; why did her throat feel choking; why did her stomach feel queasy?

Tim began to introduce her. "Ranger Molly Bishop

may look like nothing more than a pretty gal in uniform, but. . . ."

For the tenth time, she wished Gloria and Dutch were in the audience, but they were at Camp 14, running another evening program. Woodenly, she started up the steps.

Tim concluded, "May I present Molly Bishop, our ranger in skirts!"

Clapping sounded, faces smiled up at her. She adjusted the microphone and looked down at the waiting campers. Her throat went dry, her mind blank. Suddenly, a wildly grimacing boy caught her unseeing eyes. It was Foxy. Next to him was Betty Fox, smiling anxiously and encouragingly at Molly.

Although she had meant to preface the slides with general remarks on the Yosemite Indian life, she pressed the button and a picture of a cedar *umacha* flashed on the screen. She stepped aside, looked at the slide blankly, swallowed, and began speaking spontaneously.

"Your tent or trailer is a lot more comfortable and convenient than the Indian *umacha* or teepee, but it was home and hearth to them. An open fire burned in the middle, keeping everyone warm; and if the roof leaked, another cedar slab could be added easily."

Her words sounded inadequate, so she switched slides to one of intricately woven baskets holding drifts of acorns. "Acorns were the staff of life to Indians." Her voice steadied, warmed. "From oak tree to consumer was a lengthy process involving picking, cracking, shelling, pounding, leaching out the bitterness, and, finally, cooking. Those of you women who struggle with campfires can sympathize with the Indian women who bent over hot cooking baskets, lowering heated stones in with wooden tongs."

After that it became progressively easier for Molly to use illustrative words to go with the slides. Thanks to the gathering darkness and the pictures, no one looked at her; so she relaxed into the easy, factual informality that had characterized her other talks. When she was through, reassuring applause swept up.

Tim took over for the nightly firefall ceremony, and she wandered haphazardly down. Foxy grabbed her arm and pulled her around back of the stage.

Betty took both of her hands and said meaningfully, "My dear, you gave a fine talk, though you had me worried at first. I told Breck you would never survive a week's preparation and practicing on camp too."

Molly grinned, not minding the affectionate "my dear," and glad to have Gloria's suspicions confirmed.

Betty continued briskly, "We'll run along, but will you and Tim stop by the store for some more coffee, please? I'm almost out and we'll need more for campfire tonight."

"Campfire?" Molly echoed. Lately, Camp 19'ers had been meeting in the Foxes' tent.

"Campfire," Betty repeated firmly. "I expect you to be there."

"Don't worry, I wouldn't miss it." She meant every word.

Even though Molly attended and joined in companionable talk, she was uneasy. Dutch and Gloria were not there.

126

Betty said, "That's Gloria! She promised to bring whipped cream for the gingerbread, and it's way after ten now!"

Breck reearned Molly's black thoughts by saying, "Maybe they're walking in the moonlight."

Molly leaned back against a tree, her face in shadow, her mind in tumult. Of course, they might be walking together. Why not? They were old friends. Still, she had thought they would be anxious to hear about her talk.

She wondered what they were talking about. Surely Dutch didn't confide, as he had last night, often? Gloria was so very pretty, so charming, and so smart. Molly hugged her knees fiercely, seeing Gloria's clear, laughing face tilted upward toward Dutch.

"Having fun?" Tim asked gently.

"Yes," she answered hollowly, "but I am tired."

"Not too tired for Betty's whipped cream-less gingerbread, are you?" he asked, adding in a whisper, "She made it for you to celebrate."

Molly nodded. "I thought so. I won't leave."

But the gingerbread clogged her mouth and throat so that it was hard to swallow. What's wrong with me? she wondered wildly. My ordeal is over; I like these people; it's nice to have Tim attentive, yet I'm miserable. Whatever is causing it?

Then she jerked upright at the violence, the ugliness of a thought. She was jealous!

As quickly as the unbidden thought filled her mind, car doors slammed, and running footsteps pounded. "Hey, gang, guess why we're late!" Gloria's vibrant voice preceded her entrance in the camp firelight. "We've been visiting with a congressman who's on the House Committee for Interior Appropriations."

Her golden hair tumbled down, firelight lit excited blue eyes, and her face was alive with wonder. And beauty, Molly admitted, as she watched Dutch come to Gloria's side. His expression, too, was animated and flushed.

"No kidding, we had a real, live congressman in our audience complete with a cigar and rhetoric."

"A congressman camping?" Irving sounded astounded.

Dutch grinned, nodding. "Camping—roughing it in a thirty-foot trailer with his wife and family."

"He insisted on showing us every shelf and cupboard," Gloria interrupted. "After the program, he took us over. A little pompous, but a nice old dear."

Dutch carried on the explanation. "Smart too. He asked us all sorts of sharp questions about Yosemite, the wilderness concept, and the Park Service."

Gloria chuckled, then laid a casual hand on Dutch's shoulder. "The congressman made the mistake of mentioning John Muir, and our disciple here was off and talking. I thought I would never pry him off to come join Molly's party."

Molly managed a smile, but her heart was sick at the sight of her friend's hand on Dutch. Another thought struck her. If these horrid feelings stemmed from jealousy, could she be in love?

Next morning Molly was relieved to wake up normally hungry, and anticipating Junior Rangers. Life looked different, clear-cut in the early sunlight, reducing her feelings of the previous night to sheer lunacy.

Gloria confirmed the idiocy of jealousy by asking, as she flew into her clothes, "Molly, would you press my black sheath dress, pretty please? I have a date tonight with a dreamy ranger from Wawona."

Molly queried cautiously, "Don't you ever go with the same man twice?"

"Do I seem like a flirt?" Gloria countered blithely. "My innocent child, the time will come when I steady down to a one-man devotion, but there's only one man who interests me and he's far away."

Whistling, Molly left for work but first checked the assignment schedule posted on the bear baffle and then the parking lot. Dutch's pickup was gone, and he was on contact duty. She pictured him answering campers' questions calmly, but with a depth of knowledge. As usual, his hat would be cocked at an unofficial angle, his head up, eyes alert. Whenever she had been with him, his casual asides—"Look at the lichen on that rock. There's my old pal the nuthatch. From the looks of this bent grass, I'll wager a deer has been bedding down here" —had interested and impressed her.

"Hey, Ranger," Tim's gay voice punctured her reverie, "how about a date tonight?"

"Sure," she smiled back, but felt no lifting of her heart, none of the flooding excitement experienced before with Tim. "Where and what?"

"Dancing?" He saw her shudder. "No? That's right, you don't like crowds. How about dinner in Wawona?"

"Sounds like fun."

The evening was fun. After dinner, they strolled around the historic hotel buildings, revisited the Pioneer History Center, and played an exuberant game of tennis. While they had walked hand in hand and talked with surprising bursts of confidence, there was no romance or excitement.

Molly caught herself wondering what Dutch was doing. Writing, probably; possibly doing research in the library. Did he write smoothly and swiftly; or scribble, then crumple pages? Did he use a pen or a typewriter? She thought of asking Tim as they drove home since he shared a tent with Dutch. Some inner warning kept her silent. As Tim's date, he should have her attention and interest, not his roommate who thought she was so young.

Friday morning she woke before daylight when the sky was slaty, and the last stars were blinking out. On impulse, she hopped out of bed, dressed quickly, grabbed an apple and a candy bar, and bicycled off to Happy Isles. From there she could walk to Vernal Fall and back while the trail was deserted.

She needed time alone to gain perspective in her thoughts, to "climb the mountains and get the glad tidings." As she parked her bike in the wooden rack, Muir's words came to her: "Nature's peace will flow into you as sunshine flows into trees."

How appropriate! "Nature's peace" would soothe her thoughts, clarify her feelings toward Dutch, and help her see herself and Breck more clearly.

She sniffed the air for the mingled odors of blooming azaleas, pine, and river shrubs, but a scent bothered her. Smoke here where no one lived? Fire?

Her eyes dilated with apprehension. Swiftly, she trod the familiar trail toward the Junior Rangers' meeting place. A parked car faced her, momentarily halted her. No one should be here. Even early hikers would park in the large parking lot.

All she could hear was the joyful, crashing sounds of the river. A second look at the car established it as belonging to a teen-ager, for it was emblazoned with painted signs, "Yosemite or bust! Watch our dust! Look, no engine," and the like.

A stronger whiff of smoke sent her hurrying around the dark Nature Center building to a sight that horrified her.

Smoke spiraled up from a campfire tended by a husky teen-ager who was frying fish. A second boy was rolling up sleeping bags. Still, Molly's shock was not for their camping in an undesignated area nor even for their fire, but for the activities of the third boy, a hulking, muscular young man.

He was bending over the low fence around the exhibit fish pool, spearing handsome rainbow trout. As she watched, he drew a sixteen-inch trout up, turning triumphantly to his companions. "This baby's got my name on him! Boy howdy, is that going to taste good!"

Infuriated, Molly dashed forward. "Put that fish down. Can't you read? Don't you know these trout are just to show visitors and are protected by law?"

"Aw, calm down, sister." The spearman regarded appraisingly. "We spent the whole day fishing yesterday for nothing. We didn't even catch an old tin can. You know there's nothing like a fresh-caught, fresh-cooked trout, so we just spent part of the night here, and now. . . ."

"You're breaking three Park rules," she interrupted furiously, her eyes burning with intensity—"camping, starting a fire in an undesignated area, and spearing fish in front of a sign that says 'Fishing prohibited by law.'"

"What are you going to do about it?" the cook asked. "If you'll be nice, we'll give you some. Fish, fried potatoes, hot coffee—how does that sound?"

She stepped forward, grasped their camp shovel, and began spading dirt on the flames.

"Hey," the cook grabbed the frying pan, "what do you think you're doing? Stop it."

Suddenly, her arms were caught, held so tightly she cried out. Roughly, the sleeves of her sweat shirt were shoved up, her bare wrists pinioned.

"Hurt? Good!" her captor, the spearman, said grimly. "What else did you plan to do, you little trouble-maker?"

"Turn you in." She twisted violently, futilely, but his grip on her arms only tightened painfully. "I'm a Ranger-naturalist."

"Yeah," the boy with the sleeping bags guffawed, "and I'm the Park Superintendent! Why, I bet your folks will have a fit when they find you're out of their tent. A ranger, hah!"

"But I am," she protested, realizing that her protest was as futile as her struggling. Her dress was that of a camper, even the teen-ager they thought her; she had no wallet, no official identification, nothing that would establish her as a ranger. "Let me go."

132

"What are we going to do with her?" the cook asked worriedly. "No matter what she is, we're in trouble when we let her loose. Let's get out of here."

Molly looked up fearfully. Two scowling boys glared at her. They looked troubled, but the third, obviously not a teen-ager, loomed ominous and baleful. His never-relaxing grip, his angry, authoritative voice showed that he was the leader. Although the sky was light, her practiced woods eye told her that it was a long time before eight, before a naturalist would come on duty at the Nature Center. Unless a chance hiker should come by, she was at their mercy.

"If we let you go," the youngest one, the sleeping bag boy, asked, "would you promise not to report us for an hour?"

"Of course not, you sap," her captor muttered angrily.

"What would happen to us if we were caught?" the cook questioned tentatively.

"Fines, probably some time in jail, publicity." With each prophecy the leader tightened his grip on Molly's wrists convulsively. Tears sprang to her eyes, but she made no outcry. "Your fathers would be notified since you two are underage."

"Mine would kill me." "Sleeping Bag" looked stricken. "No kidding, I had to make all sorts of promises before he let me come on this camping trip."

Concern impregnated the cook's expression. "If I had to pay a fine of over twenty-five bucks, I couldn't meet my car payment and my dad would be wild with joy. He thinks my jalopy's for the birds anyway."

"We're wasting time," the leader said impatiently. "I vote we tie her up behind a rock somewhere near and skin out of here." 　　　　　　　　. .

"Right," "Sleeping Bag" agreed, pouring a bucket of water to finish putting out the fire.

While Molly watched helplessly, the two younger boys put their gear in the car, stuffed the bloody fish in a trash can, and cleaned up their campsite quickly.

The nightmare was real. Screaming would do no good; the river was too vocal. Reasoning seemed forlorn as, evidently, fathers were more frightening than rangers.

Still, she had to say something. "Tying me up will just. . . ."

"Shut up and start walking." She had to bite her lip to keep from crying out as hard hands punished her speech.

The cook regarded her bitterly. "Why did you have to come along and mess up everything?"

"Why did you break rules?" she flashed back.

After a short walk they angled off the trail into a small clearing walled by thick pines and a room-sized boulder. "This will do. Here, hold her while I tie this rope around her wrists."

"Sleeping Bag" assured her, "Someone will spot you here in an hour or so. By that time we'll be long gone." His manner and speech betrayed an inner unease at the proceedings.

Obviously, the leader was untouched by any regret or kindliness. Not only did he truss her wrists and rope her shoulders to a tree, but tied her feet securely together, then took a bandana from "Sleeping Bag's" back pocket.

"Do we need to gag her, too?" he cried protestingly.

Regarding him blackly, the leader asked, "Ever been in jail? Yes, we need to gag this big-mouthed babe." Angrily he tied the cloth so that it smoothed tightly against her mouth, compressing her lips achingly against her teeth. "There, that ought to keep you still for a while. Come on, you guys, let's orbit."

Heavy feet clumped off, but "Sleeping Bag" lingered. "Look," he mumbled sheepishly, "I'm sorry about this. I'm not what you call a juvenile delinquent; neither's my buddy. This thing just sorta happened, and now it's too late to stop it."

Imploringly, she rolled her eyes, pleading silently, "It's not too late. Untie me quick." Rope bit into her chafed skin, her wrists burned and the gag—the final, nightmarish enormity—choked her.

"Sleeping Bag" took a tentative step toward her just as the leader ran back and sneered, "Fool! If we're caught now, after tying her, the charges will really be serious. Come on."

They fled, leaving Molly in misery and near-terror occasioned by the smothering gag. Nothing else they had done had stifled her spirit as that tightly bound piece of cloth. With her lips, her jaw, her teeth, she fought it so that it loosened, but it kept her captive.

Not only did she ache physically and mentally, but the mosquitoes zeroed in, and the sun fingering the clearing turned her sweat shirt into a prison. Molly remembered all the stories of torture she had ever read—water dripping on the forehead, ants crawling on a burning desert captive—and decided that her own predicament was bearable. Indignities multiplied as time crawled by. After sneezing, she couldn't blow her nose, her stomach growled, and a squirrel-cut pine cone thudded sharply to her knee. At times tears flooded her eyes, but an inner strength staved off useless sobbing.

Minutes stretched so endlessly that it seemed she had been captive for hours, yet a careful check of the sun's position disheartened her and made her doubt that it was even nine-thirty.

Junior Rangers must be in full swing, but all she could hear was the river. Her mind fretted, someone would be searching for her, Laura, Gloria, possibly Breck. Probably not, though; her early morning jaunts had become accepted. Laura might cluck worriedly, but Gloria would say, "She's all right. What could possibly hurt her in the woods?"

Frantic, Molly thought of Breck. Surely he would be concerned; whatever her failings, she was always at work on time. From the schedule, she knew that Breck, Tim, and Irving were with the Junior Rangers; Dutch was on museum duty. Dutch—no Muir quote would come to him if he could see her now.

Again tears welled in her eyes; a few slid down her sunburning face, further demoralizing her as she could not wipe them away. Again she struggled against her rigid bonds and again they held. Blood oozed from one rope-intolerant wrist.

"Miss Bishop? Molly? Can you hear me?" Help sounded near.

"Here, here!" Her scream of relief came out a muffled whimper.

136

"Please answer!" the voice bawled out plaintively.

Frenziedly she whimpered; the sounds tore at her ears.

Silence answered her; then "Miss Bishop?" It was Darrel Black's tentative, worried tone.

She redoubled her frantic, helpless groans. A branch cracked, feet stumbled through the undergrowth; Darrel rushed around the boulder, concerned face horror-struck at the sight of her.

"Oh, no, *oh no!*" His exclamation was a heartfelt cry as he ran to her, knelt, and fumblingly untied the gag.

Freed, Molly gulped air, widened her jaw, and finally croaked huskily, "Thanks! Can you untie the ropes?"

Darrel whipped out a pocket knife, cut through the ones binding her feet first, then those around her wrists. "You're bleeding! What happened? Who did this?" Outrage shone in his tone and crimsoning face.

"Some boys I caught fishing in the exhibit pond." She tried to rise. Darrel helped her to shaky feet.

"Let me go for help," he urged. "You shouldn't try walking yet. Stay here."

"Not another second," she shuddered. "You can't imagine how . . . how blessed it is to be free! I'll be all right. I'm fine." Her husky, trembling voice confessed weakness, and she was glad to put one arm around Darrel's neck.

"Which way did they go? Did they have a car?"

"Don't ask me now," she begged. "Later. It's been forever."

"Oh," he groaned. "I *told* Ranger Fox there was something wrong when you were late. I saw your bike, but I looked in all the wrong places."

It was an effort to place her feet forward. Only her mind queried, "Didn't Breck believe you?"

Unhappily, Darrel answered her unspoken question. "He thought you were off on a hike, said you could take care of yourself! Goll-ly," the cry was anguished, "I have been looking, Molly. If *only* I'd found you sooner!"

"Don't worry," she reassured him. "The important thing is you did find me, rescued me. Thank goodness."

"Look, there's Breck's car. You climb in while I go after him."

"Don't alarm the children," she cautioned, and sank back against the seat after he helped her in. Luckily, the car was parked up and away from the Junior Ranger "campus." Molly didn't want any fuss, all she wanted was oblivion.

So when Breck came swiftly, white-faced, she stated firmly, "If you would drive me home, I want to stretch out on my bed for an hour or two. Then I'll be fine, and I'll tell you what happened."

"Still independent," he marveled aloud, pulling back the cuffs of her shirt to examine her wrists. Both were angry-red and swollen, and the skin on the left one was broken. Smeared blood surrounded the open wound.

"It probably looks worse than it is," he said gently; then explosively, "The brutes!" Hurriedly, he closed the door and climbed into the car from his side and started the engine. "Your face is all red and bitten too. I'm taking you to the hospital."

138

As they drove, she argued numbly, though it seemed difficult to form words. "No, Breck, please no. Take me to camp. Some band-aids and sleep will fix me up."

Reassuringly, he said, "It's best that we let the doctor see you first, my dear child."

With her last strength, she wounded him. "I am not a child! Why do you always have to run me?"

"Molly, Molly, I am trying to help!"

The anguish in his tone stirred her. Not wanting any more pain for or from anyone, she said wearily, "I'm sorry. I didn't mean that."

At that hospital, though things happened to her, they seemed to be happening to someone else while she observed. Her sweat shirt was removed, her face and wrists bathed, treated with something stinging, and a bandage applied to her left wrist.

Both the doctor and nurse were quick and kind, doing their work with dispatch and quiet. Once she rebelled, "I don't need a shot to sleep."

"Maybe not, but I'll make sure."

Breck protested, "Wait. I'll have to take a statement before she sleeps."

"Sorry, you can do it later. In the stunned shape her mind is in, she wouldn't make sense."

From a great distance, Molly thought how funny it was to have Breck overruled.

CHAPTER X

Something clicked. Molly opened her eyes, glimpsed trees, sky, closed them again.

Clicking noises persisted. A soothing feminine voice calmed, "You're all right, Molly. Relax."

"Betty? Where am I? What's that noise?"

"You're in the hospital, and that clicking comes from my knitting needles."

"Hospital, but why? Oh." Slowly, painfully she remembered everything, even her exhausted railing at Breck. "Oh dear, poor Breck!"

"It's all right. He understood. I must go call him now so he and a ranger from the protective staff can come question you."

A little later Molly woke again, more fully, to hear Breck question carefully, "Molly, could you tell us what happened now? This is Ranger Ted Oliver."

Breck sounded so hesitant, so regretful that she opened her eyes, pulled herself into a sitting position, and winced from the pain in her wrists. Managing a smile, she assured him, "Don't worry, Breck. I'm as tough as a mountain hemlock, and I'll be glad to tell you about this morning. I set out early, around five, for Vernal Fall, but a scent of smoke. . . ."

Briefly, omitting details of her misery, she told them of her adventure. Twice, muttered exclamations escaped Breck.

Molly concluded, "I stayed tied up until Darrel found me."

Ranger Oliver questioned her further. "What kind of a car did they have?"

"An ancient jalopy. No, I didn't think to check the license for state or number." Mentally, she saw the painted signs, but held back that identifying information.

"What did these young toughs look like?"

"That's just it, they weren't toughs. At least, two of them were average teen-agers, seventeen or eighteen. Even though they were frightened and in a hurry, they broke camp with care and stamped out their fire which, by the way, was surrounded by a cleared firebreak."

"How were they dressed? Any peculiar physical characteristics?"

For ten minutes she answered his sharp questions, somewhat reluctantly. Tired, she slid back onto pillows Betty plumped behind her head.

Ranger Oliver stood. "*If,* by some miracle, these boys are caught, would you prefer charges?"

"I would hate to."

Breck said urgently, "Molly, are you sure? That was sheer torture they put you through."

She nodded, trying not to remember the muffling gag, the mosquito's hum, the deadness in her feet, her raw wrists. "I know, but as the youngest boy said, they weren't juvenile delinquents; and I'll wager neither he nor the other teen-ager ever break a law again."

"You are charitable, Miss Bishop," Ranger Oliver stated, "charitable and brave, but remember you are a federal officer and it is *your duty* to report anything that would help in capturing those boys." He looked at her searchingly. "Even if you could dismiss their assault on you, remember that they broke other Park regulations."

The room was still with all eyes on her. Molly reconsidered, thinking of her job, her pride in it, and her love of the Park that had been so outraged that morning. "I did notice a few things about the car," she confessed. "It was a black sedan, at least fifteen years old, with signs painted on it like "Yosemite or Bust!" "Look, No Engine," and "Watch Our Dust." That's really all I saw."

Ranger Oliver wrote carefully, checked the wordage with her, and had her sign the complaint. "Now," he said firmly, "we have something to pass on to the California Highway Patrol, but so much time has elapsed, it will be difficult to catch the car. Good-bye and thanks."

As he walked out, Dutch strode in. "Molly girl, are you all right?"

Happily, she sat up, but she noted the furrowed lines in his forehead, the deeper ones beside his tight, grim lips. "Fine, Dutch." Weight on her wrists caused a grimace that made her words a lie.

"Can you tell me about it? Your poor face!"

In his hand, she saw a thin book. Was he bringing

her John Muir for comfort? Her heart lurched. He cared!

Breck rescued her. "I'll tell him." Savagely, he did, and Molly resolved never to dislike Breck again; for his worried face, his heavy, emotion-rough voice showed his caring, his bitter sorrow for having taken her absence from work so lightly.

Dutch's expression tightened into grim inscrutability as he listened. When Breck concluded, he turned to Molly.

"Couldn't you have run back for help when you first saw the boys?"

"It never occurred to me," she admitted honestly. "I suppose so." She shrugged wearily and saw a fleeting look—disappointment? understanding? disgust?—touch Dutch's face.

"If only you had!" His free hand balled into a fist.

"I'm sorry." She fell back on the pillows.

Breck shook his head at Dutch. "Hindsight is always better than foresight."

"Of course," Dutch said quickly, placing the book beside her. "You were fine. I'm proud of you." He gave her a funny little salute, turned and left.

Molly closed her eyes, thinking that he was disappointed in her, once more judging her too young.

When next she woke, she was hungry and restless. Her sun sense was frustrated by being on the north, shady side of the hospital. She turned over to see Betty still there. "Thanks for staying with me," she spoke quietly. "What time is it? May I have something to eat?"

Betty smiled. "Hurrah, you're on the mend. It's just five and dinner is being served."

"Do I have to stay here? Can't I go home?"

"Not till after dinner, and maybe not then. It depends on you." Betty's appraising glance was firm, calm, and motherly.

"I'm fine now, really. Why the maybe?" Molly swung her feet off the high bed, stood and stretched, luxuriating in the freedom of motion. "See? There's nothing wrong with me that food, lots of food, won't cure in a hurry."

Betty countered, "What do you plan to do this evening?"

"Retrieve my bike, go to Irving's campfire talk, and finish up some ironing for Gloria."

"Oh no, you don't, or you stay right here all night."

"All night! Why?"

"Because today I'm taking your mother's place, and because the doctor left it up to me to decide whether or not you'd rest enough at camp. Your system had such a nervous shock, he says, you'd need twelve hours more rest to recuperate.

"Stop glaring at me, and look in the mirror."

"Gosh," Molly voiced shock at her pale, mottled image. Her hair was wild, face pocked with bites; and there were red lines from the gag around her mouth. "What a mess!"

Betty said lightly, "A vast improvement over this noon, believe me! Your eyes were dull, your face blank, and you didn't know me when I fed you."

"Did you? Betty, you are a dear." Molly marveled at the other's care and at her own amazing dependence.

"All right, tell me what I have to do to get out of here and back to dear old Camp 19."

"Let Laura and Gloria—incidentally, they're crazy to see you—wait on you, rest, read, and be in bed by nine-thirty."

"Outside?" Their eyes met, locked, argued.

"You're incorrigibly independent. Outside then."

"Yes, 'Mother.' "

Camp visitors interrupted Betty's planned, restful evening until Molly herself called a halt. "Please," she told Rowena and Marcy. "Don't ask me about it. I don't want to think about it any more. It was horrible."

Understandingly, the women left, but Tim, Foxy, Gloria, and Laura were all in the front tent where Molly sat upright in a chair, wanting to run outside, yet not knowing how to dismiss herself from the surrounding kindness. She craved the solitude she had been searching for since daylight.

Conversation, even about nature, irritated her. Sunday and Monday were her days off. Perhaps she could escape to the vast and lonely grandeur around Tuolumne Meadows.

Betty came in, glanced sharply at her and announced, "Curfew. Off to bed with you."

With alacrity, Molly was on her feet. "A shower first?" She knew it was nowhere near nine-thirty, and was grateful for Betty's early authoritative intervention.

"Surely you aren't going to sleep outside tonight?" Laura cried. "Aren't you afraid after this morning?"

"No," Molly said shortly; then seeing dawning hurt on Laura's face, added comfortingly, "After this morning I prize freedom even more highly. To me, sleeping ouside means freedom. You should try it."

"I'd love to." Wistfulness sounded. "You know I have never slept outside or been camping in my life."

"Never?" Molly was astounded. "Never felt the warmth of a campfire or seen the wide, starry night from a sleeping bag, or smelled bacon frying in the cold, fresh air of morning?"

"Never. Last summer here, I bought a sleeping bag, pack, boots, and a camp cot, but I'm not brave enough to camp alone like you. . . ." Laura's voice trailed off.

Impulsively, Molly stated, "I'll take you camping next time I go."

"Do you mean it? Oh, Molly, I'd love it! At work today," Laura remembered, "I copied a comment for you that P. T. Barnum, the circus king, wrote in 1870 about Yosemite. He said it was "unsurpassed and unsurpassable —look around with pleasure and upward with gratitude.' "

"Oh," Molly was thrilled. "How true. My feelings exactly. Thank you, Laura." She walked toward the showers, thinking that not even Muir could have expressed appreciation better.

Betty came out, caught up with her, and said. "Here's some hot chocolate, and a piece of cake to speed you to sleep, my dear."

"Thanks." Molly accepted food and endearment with sincerity.

One more surprise awaited her on her bed. Light

showed it to be a cedar-carved, simulated Medal of Honor. Printed in Dutch's bold, uncompromising hand, the accompanying scroll read in part, ". . . presented for courage beyond her years. . . ."

Tears smarted in Molly's eyes. Was that all he thought about? Her age? Did he think of her only as a lovable but immature girl?

Early Saturday morning, Breck met her by the bear baffle. "You look better." His joviality seemed strained.

"Don't lie," she said. "I just looked in the mirror. Ugh!" She summoned courage. "Please don't misunderstand me, Breck, but I can't face desk duty today."

He nodded. "That's what Betty and I decided, so I spoke to Irving and he's willing to trade your Monday off for his Saturday. As far as the Park Service is concerned, you are free of duty until Monday morning."

"Oh, Breck, wonderful. Thanks."

"I suppose you'll take off within minutes? Would you mind if I ask where?"

She laughed at his elaborate care not to offend her usual bristling independence. "I'm going to Tuolumne Meadows, Sierra Club campground, and I imagine Laura will go along." Inwardly she sighed. "How about my borrowing Foxy too?"

"Fine and . . ." he hesitated, troubled and indecisive.

"Go ahead. I won't bite," she teased.

"Well, you won't like my advising you, but please take it easy for a change. Don't chase bears or try to arrest lawbreakers or climb a glacier. And another thing, my de—Molly, I think you should write and tell your parents about yesterday."

A little resentfully, Molly agreed. "Yes, 'Father.' "

What with Laura's fluttery excitement, her insistence on taking a cot and mattress—"I'm too old to sleep on the ground"—and buying steaks, it was midmorning before the trio was ready to leave. Then, as Molly was pressing the starter, trying to be polite and hating herself for encumbering a camping trip with Laura, she remembered the postponed Coulterville Road trip slated for Monday.

Newly dismayed, she raced to Dutch's tent, scrawled an explaining note, and left it. It irritated her further that her words were not remotely clever or warm as his had been.

On the drive to Tuolumne Meadows, Laura had to stop at every scenic view turnoff to take pictures and read the explanatory signs aloud. Only her obvious delight in the spectacular, high country surroundings, and her oft-spoken pleasure, "You can't imagine how thrilled I am to be going camping at last," prevented Molly from asking her to be quiet.

Once Foxy caught her eyes and rolled his wildly so that she knew she didn't suffer alone.

Finally she bumped her car along a track on a rising flat bearing hardy grass, wild flowers, scattered boulders, and relatively short lodgepole pine trees. "Here we are." She piled out of the car as she made the relieved announcement. "I fell in love with this campsite when I saw it last month."

"But there's no stove or table." Laura looked as if

life were unimaginable without such conveniences.

"There's a rock campfire, and we'll improvise a table," Molly assured her. "Remember, Laura, we're roughing it. This isn't Camp 19, but the views make up for inconveniences. Look."

To their south the vividly green meadow was river-slashed, and dominated by proud, rearing granite peaks that Molly named for her, "Cockscomb, Unicorn Peak, and Cathedral Peak."

"The names fit." Laura was enthusiastic, "Especially Cathedral Peak. What are those lovely, gnarled, cinnamon-colored trees? Are they a type of cedar?"

"No, but Sierra junipers are frequently confused with cedar trees."

While Laura stood helplessly by or, worse, tried to help, Molly and Foxy blew up air mattresses, set up Laura's cot and real mattress, and fixed one canvas tarp for a windbreak.

"Laura, I'm sure you would sleep a lot warmer on the ground without cold air beneath you."

"Oh dear no. I detest crawling insects, and shouldn't sleep a wink for fretting."

"Here, I'll lay a fire for your tea. I'm an old hand at campfires."

"No, no. I intend to pull my own weight" (cough, cough) . "You know the old saying—where there's smoke there's fire—and I'm certainly making a lot of smoke."

Time and again, Molly had to grit her teeth to keep from rudely stopping Laura's ineffectual help. When Laura produced a hot-water bottle, "for warm feet to-night," Molly was only grateful the older woman hadn't expected an electrical outlet in the nearest lodgepole pine.

Oblivious to her uselessness, Laura wagged a finger after lunch. "Now I insist that you take a nap. Your face is drawn and gray again, which shows you haven't recovered from yesterday."

Foxy rolled his eyes as Molly plunked down on an air mattress. Her tiredness, except for vague achings, came, she was convinced, from the day with Laura. The night and day ahead stretched endlessly.

"I'll wander off and collect some wood for tonight while you rest. Foxy, dear, you can help me."

Foxy muttered, "She's weird!"

"Bear with her," Molly sighed. "At least, she's having a good time. Please keep an eye on her so she doesn't get lost."

Left alone, she reflected on her fortitude, thinking that her stock of patience had surely increased since Laura had first asked her to dinner. If you only could see it, Dutch, she addressed him mentally, I'm growing up.

Above, the sky arched a deep, incredible blue. She looked "around with pleasure and upward with gratitude," then fell asleep.

Several times that evening she had to calm Foxy down with her eyes, a frown, or a murmured aside, as his patience with Laura stretched thin. Molly's own annoyance mingled with amusement and anticipation at what the woman could bungle next.

A yellow jacket swooped low and Laura knocked over a pan of hot water, dousing the fire. Just as it was well started again, she set it to smoking by shoving on too much wood. "Oh dear, and I was only trying to help!"

She managed to drop the bar of soap into ashes, mislay the flashlight, and trip over a root in the darkness.

Finally, Molly could take it no longer. "Laura, remember 'when the mule kicks you once, shame on the mule, but if he kicks you twice, shame on you'? Well, you and camping are like that. Please, just sit down and watch while Foxy and I finish the chores."

Surprisingly, Laura laughed, confirming Molly's feelings by saying, "My, how you have changed since summer began. Now, I'm the one that's being mulish and you're patience itself!"

Despite that admission, Laura stuck the zipper in her sleeping bag, and insisted on putting her hair up in curlers by lantern light.

"Your head will be cold," Molly worried. "It's 8,600 feet elevation here."

"Oh no, see my stocking cap?" It was a hideous affair of orange and brown wool. "Don't you fret about my being cold. I have a flannel nightgrown, a pair of tights, my bathrobe, mittens, bedsocks, and a muffler."

"I doubt if she can squeeze into her sleeping bag," Foxy chortled.

"Just for that, young man, you can zip me in."

Even after her incarceration, Laura kept them amused. "What's that noise? Only the wind. Are you sure it wasn't a bear? What was that?"

"An owl saying good night, Laura."

Eventually snores succeeded worries, and Foxy and Molly began to compare notes. "She's so horrible, she's funny," Foxy subsided.

"Yes and well-meaning. Everything she says or does

is sincere. I think we can survive another day." Molly drew her sleeping bag up to her neck, leaving only her face exposed to the increasingly cold breeze, and her eyes free to take in the brilliance of stars. Camp 19 was good; Yosemite Valley, wonderful; but there was no place comparable to this high Sierra country with its wind-swept grandeur and unenclosed wilderness.

Sunday passed tolerably. They attended an outdoor church service conducted by a student minister, then walked through the sprawling, tent-populated public campground.

Laura was indignant. "Why didn't we camp here? Look, each campsite has a picnic table, a nice stove; there's piped water near, and washhouses with inside plumbing."

In turn, Molly was indignant. "But our campsite has far better views and a unique history. Jean Baptiste Lembert homesteaded there in 1885, and grazed Angora goats around and on our campsite."

"Oh yes, I've read about him. Wasn't he murdered near El Portal?"

Molly nodded assent. "Eventually, his Tuolumne homestead became the property of the Sierra Club, and is used as a camping place for Sierra Clubbers like me. That granite dome ahead of us was named Lembert Dome after our hero. How about climbing it this afternoon?"

"It doesn't look very high," Laura complained. "I'd like to be able to tell them that I hiked Mt. Dana."

Foxy rolled his eyes, and Molly speculated on Laura's possible condition after hiking to Mt. Dana's 13,052-foot top. Probably she and Foxy could manage it, but Laura, whose summer exercise had been limited to strolls around the Valley, was in no physical shape to tackle it.

"Camp 19 will be impressed if you tell them you hiked Lembert." She put enthusiasm in her tone. "The summit is 9,400 feet."

"But we start at 8,600," Laura stated. "Oh well, you're the boss. I bet John Muir would have led me on a longer hike."

Once they began their climb around the back shoulder of the dome, Laura settled down to taking pictures and asking questions. Molly began to enjoy herself. "Yes, that's a Sierra juniper, and that tree to our right is a mountain hemlock, *Tsuga mertensiana.*"

"Ah ha, I know that one from my reading." Laura stopped, removed the new back pack she had insisted on carrying, and dug into it for a book. "My memory isn't photographic like our friend Dutch's, but I'm sure Muir said the hemlock was the most beautiful conifer he'd ever seen."

Waiting, Molly gazed affectionately at Laura, who was dressed strangely in wool slacks, a purple knit pullover, and huge dark glasses. Around her thin neck hung a camera and a light meter, a canteen was strapped to her wide belt, and a large, floppy straw hat topped the hiking outfit.

In contrast, Molly's attire—jeans, a short-sleeved T-shirt, and small pack—was simple and lightweight.

Slowly, their climb continued. Molly suspected that their frequent stops were to allow Laura to rest, although she leafed through a book or fiddled with her camera as well as panted. While such slowness irritated Foxy, Molly studied her much-creased topographic map in relation to the rugged country, made notes, and wished that Dutch were along.

Any experienced naturalist could have given them the background behind such evident glacial action as glacial polish and erratic boulders; but Dutch, with his love of the Sierra and warm human history background, would have been a perfect guide.

From the glacial-weathered top of Lembert, spectacular views awed all of them. From her pack Laura produced binoculars which she passed around silently. Pretty soon, she gave them chocolate bars.

"What else do you have in that pack of yours?" Molly asked in amazement.

"I came prepared for emergencies." Proudly, Laura drew things from her pack. "A first aid kit, snake bite kit, canned water, pemmican, fishing line, hooks, plastic raincoat, soap, washrag, towel, extra socks, flashlight, waterproofed matches, pocket knife, toilet paper, nuts . . ."

"Stop, stop." Foxy lay back on the granite overcome with laughter.

Laura was hurt. "I thought all mountaineers carried such provisions."

"They do, and I do," Molly tried to keep a straight face, "on a long back-packing trip, but from here you can see our camp, the store, and ranger station."

Laura pulled a last item from her Pandora's box, and said with great dignity, "Nevertheless, if I hadn't brought along my canned heat, we shouldn't be able to brew tea."

CHAPTER XI

By Monday morning Molly's aches were healed, face presentable, and she went back to work with zeal. As always, the Junior Ranger program was stimulating and rewarding, and she found the job even more enjoyable since she and Breck were on good terms.

She rode to Happy Isles and back with him, discussed matters with him, and even lunched with the Foxes. Breck had a shelf full of books and pamphlets on mammals, birds, bushes, and flowers of the Sierra. His brain was packed with information on nature subjects that he delighted in sharing with her.

His invariable pomposity and kindly phrasing "Now, my dear, if you'll just notice," no longer angered her. When he criticized her independent actions, she listened quietly, sometimes modified her plans or, if not, didn't defy him.

Scrutinizing her one noon, he said heavily, "It's high time you prepared another slide talk."

"But Breck, I know Indians better than anything."

"Of course, but giving it twice a week from now till Labor Day is going to be mighty boring. Besides, I can't schedule it that often as the average camper stays ten days and wants to know something different."

Twice a week was all she had heard and that echoed frighteningly in her head. "Twice a week from now on?"

"Yes, I'm going to schedule you as I do any of the men naturalists, giving a talk twice, hosting a program one night, and showing a Yosemite film another night."

Betty spoke up in an amused tone. "You shouldn't look so dismayed. After all, Breck is paying you the compliment of considering you equal to the men."

"Yes, but all those people four nights a week and a new talk. . . ."

Breck laughed. "You can face them as well as a bear or law-breakers, Missy. I have great faith in you."

She saw her advantage. "Then put me on regular contact duty as you do the other men."

"No, I don't want you wandering through campgrounds alone. There are too many two-legged wolves, and you're so impulsive and. . . ."

Without argument she let him rant on, keeping her eyes on his the whole time.

Eventually, he blustered, "Oh, all right, I'll let you try once more."

"When? This afternoon? We could trade duties. You can take mine at the museum, and I'll take yours at Camp 15."

He beetled his brows at her. "What do you do, memorize my schedule?"

No, she replied silently, but I know Dutch's by heart.

"You tour Camp 15 then today, but don't be impetuous. If someone has a caged squirrel, call the museum for directions. I mean that."

Breck's fears were groundless. Though a few boys whistled admiringly at her, the afternoon was routine and question-filed. It was routine except that the questioners were outdoors, and instead of referring to a book, took her to the tree, flower, or bush they wanted identified. Children, mostly Junior Rangers, tagged her. "Hey, Ranger Molly, here's an animal track."

Beside a crumpled cigarette package, she spied a raccoon print, so she picked up the trash and explained the print; then she had an idea. "Hey, gang, have you ever heard of the American litterbug—a strange, two-legged mammal? Let's trail some and pick up their droppings."

Before long she had a trail of enthusiastic youngsters picking up trash left by careless campers. Some ran back to campsites for paper sacks; others unburdened their hands at the frequent trash cans.

At first they were lighthearted—"Hurrah, comic books!" "Look, a bicycle pump." "Here's some more cola cans."

Soon, she heard scorn and disgust creep into their voices. "Look at all the broken glass! And the trash can's only five feet away." "Can you imagine leaving goopy old stockings around?" "Cigarette butts all over the place! Ugh." "That's nothing—here's a whole banged-up bedsprings." "People are terrible!"

Molly smiled, satisfied. Without a word from her, a lot of children were learning firsthand about litterbugs and human erosion. Their sense of conservation had been aroused, and she bet they'd all be more careful about throwing things away. As a reward she led them on a short nature walk through an adjoining meadow. Several adults came along.

"What do you suppose this old, decaying log is good for?" she began, wondering if the adults would be bored at the simplicity of her approach. The large, barkless pine log with its holes and gray age held everyone's attention.

"Fire wood?" a man suggested.

"Oh, Daddy!" a disgusted girl cried; then turned to Molly. "Is it kind of an apartment house for bees and termites?"

"Right. It's air conditioned, rent free, and not too close to human neighbors. What could it be doing that's beneficial to the meadow?"

It was interesting to watch expressions, Molly thought. Most of the children were thinking visibly as if facial contortions might help brain work. In contrast, nearly all the adults were watching her blankly, waiting for an answer. Rather than simply supplying answers, she knew that interpretation meant making the Park meaningful to visitors. Often this was accomplished by raising questions in their minds.

A thin boy who had to hold his bathing trunks up over a nonexistent waist had an idea. "Maybe the log's decaying sort of fertilizes the meadow. Kind of like humus building up the soil."

Molly chose her words with care. "As a result

158

of the decay, which takes many, many years, the soil is loosened, replenished, and made ready to bring forth more plant life. The forest is always in a continuous and wonderful pattern of growth, death, decay, and rebirth."

Bicycling back to camp, Molly was well pleased with her pleasant afternoon. If Dutch or Breck were just in camp, she would tell them about it. Unhappily for her confiding mood, there wasn't a male in camp over Foxy's age. Dutch had a free evening as did she. If only he would ask her for another walk. If only they could talk.

Then she remembered that her free evening had best be devoted to working up a new talk. While she read and made copious, uninspired notes, Breck stopped in.

Breck wanted to hear of her contact duty and, reluctantly, approved it. "I suppose I'll have to schedule you again." As he was leaving, he said, "Why don't you come on over to the tent with me? The clan is beginning to gather, and Betty mentioned something about cookies."

"Not tonight, thanks."

"But we're friends now! Don't tell me you're still going to be antisocial?"

In dismay, she saw the familiar hurt look creep into his face. "I'd like to come, truly, but my mean old boss has ordered me to dream up a new talk."

He grinned. "I hear he's a regular Simon Legree."

In the two hours alone after that Molly read, thought, and listed possible subjects. Human history? No, Dutch and Dale Hudson took care of that. Mammals? Gloria had a good talk on them; Tim covered fish and birds. Irving had the geology slide talk sewed up; Breck alternated with the "Seasons of Yosemite," "Hiking

Half Dome," and a wild flower talk. What was left? Gloria dashed in, flung clothes about, and rushed out. "I smell coffee, and you look forbidding. So long."

Molly doodled, and her mind slipped to Dutch. Where had he been all evening? Was he in the Foxes' tent? Would he ask about her? Maybe Breck would talk approvingly of her work in the campground to Dutch.

Laura came in blithely. "What's your subject?"

"I wish I knew!" Molly cradled her chin with her hands. "All the logical topics are taken—birds, fish, mammals—there's nothing left."

"There must be something you haven't thought of yet," Laura protested, clearing off the table for tea things. "Why, I'm sure you've overlooked something."

Molly was annoyed at Laura calmly assuming knowledge of nature after so recently showing an amazing ignorance of everything.

"I know a subject that no one is using this summer."

"What?" asked Molly.

"Trees of Yosemite. They're mentioned in all the talks, but why not devote your whole time to them?"

Sourness vanished from Molly's mind as ideas began to churn. "Why not indeed? Let's see, it could begin something like this: 'Only God can make a tree,' flash a slide on of a giant sequoia, 'but only man can protect it.' Show a group of awed visitors looking up at a sequoia. Then I could tell briefly about the wisdom shown by men in 1864 when the Mariposa Grove and Yosemite Valley were set aside as a public trust in which every living thing was preserved in its natural state."

"Good. Excellent." Absently, Laura held the teapot,

saying, "Then you could show color slides of different trees with some explanation about each one. Why, if they turn out well, you could use some of the slides I took on our camping trip."

Molly sprang up. "Laura, you are a dear! You have saved my professional neck. What other references should I read besides Tressidder, Cole, and Brockman?"

"Why, Muir of course. Perhaps you could preface your remarks with some of his words like that wonderful bit about the mountain hemlock. What did he say? 'But the best words only hint at its charms. Come to the mountains and see.' "

"Do you suppose Dutch would mind? After all, Muir is his man."

"Of course he won't mind! All he does is try to spread the Muir gospel. Ask him."

Glad of an excuse to speak to Dutch, Molly caught up with him the following afternoon when he came in the training room after contact duty.

"Hi, Molly. I just came from Camp 15, and some of the youngsters there informed me in no uncertain terms that I didn't fill your naturalist's shoes. Congratulations, you really put in some lasting licks for conservation."

As her chest swelled with pride, she felt her heart speed up. Was she imagining it or did his face show affection? Or was it the same look he gave little children?

"Thanks, and now I have a question about a new talk I'm organizing." Briefly she outlined it. "So I wondered if you would mind if I quoted Muir?"

"Mind? Why, I'm delighted. Your talk will be a natural. Muir and trees go together like pine cones and pitch. I should have thought of the idea myself."

Sorry to dissuade him of her unoriginality, she admitted ruefully, "Laura gave me the subject."

"Did she? That was a splendid thing you did for her last weekend. She's been bending my ear ever since concerning the glories of camping out. From things she's let drop, I think you exhibited great forbearance in not drowning her in the river."

Pleasure threatened to choke Molly, and flooded her face with a blush. He was noticing and approving the changes in her! "I did think of that, but I'm glad I stuck it out."

"Good enough. If you have time now, let's go check the slide file for possibilities. By the way, the sugar pine was Muir's favorite conifer. He said, 'The Sugar Pine is king, surpassing all others, not merely in size but in lordly beauty and majesty. . . . No tree lover will ever forget his first meeting with the sugar pine.' "

Dutch snorted at the slide file on trees. "There must be ten slides on ponderosa pines, but I don't find one of the knobcone or the singleleaf pinyon pine. Never mind, maybe we can shoot those Monday when we go on our much-postponed trip. You haven't changed your mind, have you?"

"No," Molly grinned.

During her limited free time, Molly wrote and cut, revised and cut, trying to work her talk into its allotted half hour. "I'd like to try it out on camp Friday night, then do more revision before Tuesday when you have scheduled me for its public debut. May I?"

Breck teased, "From the attention you're giving this talk, you might think it was going to be nationally broadcast. Friday will be fine. It will be nice to have you join us."

She ignored the slight sarcasm and wondered if the camp would criticize her talk the way they had Gloria's. On nature walks she was able to incorporate parts of her talk to her group of Junior Rangers. Not surprisingly, they were far less impressed with the fact that true cedars grew in Syria, Asia Minor, and the Himalaya Mountains than that incense-cedar wood was used in making pencils. Clued, Molly crumpled her description for a lighter-veined rewrite including the pencil reference and an exchange with the children. When she had asked, "What is the value of an incense-cedar?" answers had poured in.

"Cedar chests and pencils are made from the wood."

"It's valuable because it smells good."

"Woodpeckers use it to store acorns."

"Sometimes bats live in the holes."

A little, pony-tailed girl stated decisively, "It's nice to look at!"

Friday night came, and so did all the adults in camp to gather around a campfire to hear Molly. At first she spoke hesitantly, but Laura's good slides, Muir's helpful words, and her own love of trees swept her along.

Enthusiastically, she concluded, "Trees have many noncommercial and valuable purposes for being preserved in a National Park. They provide shade and shelter for smaller herbaceous plants; their cones provide food for many rodents; their roots help control erosion and hold soil together like a sponge, thereby building a healthy watershed; their needles and leaves replenish the earth; and, best of all, trees uplift the heart and soul because, as the Junior Ranger put it, they're nice to look at!"

The Camp 19'ers rewarded her with vigorous applause.

Breck spoke up. "I hate to be the one to apply cold water, Molly, but your talk is far too long."

Gloria agreed. "About twenty minutes too long."

"Yes," Irving voiced a criticism, "and too fast."

Molly, not wanting anyone to think she couldn't take criticism, hoped her face didn't mirror her dismay. "I thought I had cut my descriptions of each tree pretty short, but I'll take up my red pencil again."

"That's not the answer," Laura cried. "Not being a naturalist, I'm more representative of the people you'll be addressing, and I liked every word even though you went too fast. Can't you cut out some of the forest so we can see the trees?"

"Laura's right," Dutch approved warmly. "Your problem is you're covering too broad a field by talking about pines and broad-leaved trees like maples and oaks. They don't belong in your talk."

"Yes, but if I just dwell on cone-bearing trees," Molly objected, "won't my talk be too short?"

"No," Breck said, "because you can slow down, and let your gasping audience relax and appreciate each tree. That will polish a very fine and meaningful talk."

164

Saturday noon Molly took a letter and two package claim checks from her post office box. Since Saturday was a half day, she couldn't claim and examine them. As she stared at the fat envelope, addressed in her mother's handwriting, she realized, abruptly, that Monday would be her twentieth birthday! That explained packages. Twenty! At last she would be out of her teens. Marveling, she sat on the sun-heated post office steps.

Her high spirits drooped a little as she decided that there was no one with whom to share her momentous news. After all her boycotting of Camp 19 parties, how could she mention, casually, that her birthday was coming? If Gloria and Laura knew, they would make a great fuss and rush out to buy gifts.

Better to keep it quiet; she made the decision feeling slightly noble and self-sacrificing. Anyway, Monday would be special because of the trip with Dutch, Tim, and Foxy. With that thought, she forgot everything else except Dutch.

Gloria broke her reverie by running up the steps asking, "Are you worrying about your old trees again? Wait till I retrieve my mail and I'll treat you to a hamburger."

Moments later she was back, exclaiming, "Guess what, the fellow I date a lot during the school year is coming to the Park Saturday. Good grief, that's today! He wants to spend Sunday with me. Listen: '*so I can see what lures you from town and me three months of the year.*' Oh, dear, I work all day tomorrow." Gloria managed to look beguiling, yet woebegone, as she gazed significantly at Molly.

"I'll substitute," Molly said sturdily, thinking if she were working, she would have little time to think about her tree talk or Dutch.

"Will you? You are a doll! Come on to the coffee shop where my gratitude shall turn into steak rather than a hamburger."

"Do you ever save any money?" Molly marveled, conscious of Gloria's constant generosity to everyone in camp plus appearing almost weekly with new clothes from the dress shop.

Gloria shook her head firmly. "Not in the summer—that's my fun time."

"How about winter?"

"You wouldn't know me; I bank every other nickel toward putting my brother through college, and helping me through life."

"You are a nut!" Though her words were flippant, Molly's affection and admiration sounded.

"Don't look now," Gloria countered in equal sincerity, "but you are in eminent danger of becoming a first-class nut yourself."

Molly smiled, thinking that Gloria had given her the best birthday present she could possibly receive—an accolade of maturity.

A man saluted the glow on Molly's face. "Nice day, isn't it?"

"Wonderful," she agreed.

"Molly Bishop," Gloria stage-whispered a few steps farther on. "You just talked to "a people." I thought you were afraid of people."

"I was, I am; but Yosemite visitors, most of them

anyway, are special people." Molly attempted to put her new feelings into words. "Lately I've been noticing how friendly people look, especially when you see them on trails. They look like smiling; and I think it is because they're full of wonder and awe, and they want to share their feelings."

Gloria said gravely, "After that profound speech, I christen thee Sister Nut."

CHAPTER XII

A breeze swept Molly's face and sleepy eyes on the dawn of her twentieth birthday. For a while she lay still, savoring nature scents and thinking that calendar age had little to do with mental and emotional maturity. That was coming to her with difficulty, and with the demands of interdependent camp life.

Parties, presents, and cake celebrating a birth date meant nothing if a person acted impulsively and selfishly. Such long thoughts sent her flying out of bed to make hearty lunches for Dutch, Tim and Foxy who had been invited along.

Part of the trip she and Tim rocketed along in the back of Dutch's pickup; part of the time she squeezed in the cab with Dutch and Foxy; the rest of the time she walked with them, exploring happily, along the hill-hugging Coulterville Road.

Their first stop was on a sunny ridge thickly blanketed with mountain misery, Brodiea.

"Picture stop," Dutch announced, and stepped out laden down with two cameras, a light meter, and a tripod.

Molly looked about for something unique to photograph, and spotted a pine tree that literally sprouted cones from its slender trunk. "So this is the old knobcone pine that grows sparsely and never drops cones."

"It does after forest fires," Dutch corrected, taking a light reading. "In 1936 fire blackened this ridge, but what knobcones were here then germinated new growth as the intense heat caused the cones to open and discharge their seeds."

"The tree with built-in fire insurance," Tim suggested. "There's a flock of them growing around here now."

"Yes, this is one of the four places these trees occur in Yosemite. Because of their isolation, visitors rarely see them, so a good slide and some words of description should add interest to your tree talk, Ranger Bishop."

Both men had collecting permits; and beyond the Park boundary, Molly too was free to pick up rock specimens, and gnarled manzanita pieces. At first, carrying only a notebook, pencil, and camera, she had laughed at her burdened companion, but later she was sorry she was not equally equipped.

Besides photographic equipment, Dutch wore a backpack containing plant press, binoculars, a notebook, and a weighty volume on California flora. Tim was burdened with cameras, botany plant key, magnifying glass, and collecting bag.

Only Foxy was unencumbered to range widely, unenthused by clumps of shrubs. From each sortie he dragged back, shirt stuck with twigs, socks studded with foxtails, pockets heavy with rocks, and hands full of various treasures—a hunk of obsidian, sugarpine cones, and once a perfect set of deer antlers.

Molly studied, took notes and pictures, observed animal tracks in the road, and became so absorbed and content she almost forgot Dutch's presence.

Sometimes she merely gazed, eyes swallowing the expanse of timber, plunging, brush-sided canyons, sharp, distant mountain ranges, and vast, vast blue sky. Invariably, the old stagecoach road wound in and out on the sunny south side of the mountains; invariably, there were vistas—lawn-like mountain misery, park-like pines slicing into the sky, and exciting wilderness.

Once Dutch paused with her. Sunburn mounted his fair cheeks, his faded blue shirt was open at the collar, and his blue eyes were far from glacial. As they smiled at her, they were lively, personal, almost tender. "Happy?"

There were no ready words to express her content, her oneness with the day, the good-smelling world, and being with him. She nodded, wishing he knew and liked the root cause of her content. Shyly, she said, "I have a Yosemite quote for you to fit this day."

"Muir?"

"No, Phineas T. Barnum. 'Unsurpassed and unsurpassable—look around with pleasure and upward with gratitude.' "

Impulsively Dutch hugged her.

At lunch near a sunny, splashing waterfall that seemed completely private, Dutch told them some of the road's history. "It was completed from the gold-mining town of Coulterville to Yosemite Valley in June, 1874, a scant month before the rival Big Oak Flat Road was finished and began siphoning away traffic and tolls."

Molly watched swarming ladybugs dart over Indian rhubarb plants, and the granite-held pools of water splinter and ripple under Foxy's hurled rocks.

Six miles and eight botanizing stops beyond the fall, they came to the Merced Grove of Big Trees, grand, infinitely-reaching sequoias.

"Odd," Molly mused; "these giants are awe-inspiring yet not so overwhelming as those at the Mariposa Grove. Why?"

Tim answered thoughtfully, "There are fewer trees here, only thirty or forty instead of six hundred, and they're scattered along the creek in this friendly valley instead of over acres and acres of timbered mountainside."

Dutch continued, "Here the growth is different and much heavier than in the relatively bare Mariposa Grove. Just look around—lush ferns, grasses, dogwoods, azaleas, columbines, thick chinquapin, deer brush; and the ground is littered with needles, cones, branches, rotting logs—wilderness refuse."

Foxy spoke up. "I know why it's different. No people, no cars, not even a tunnel tree to drive through."

"Right," Tim agreed. "No human litter, voices or footsteps. This is a private part of Yosemite, alone, unspoiled, and largely unappreciated."

"Thank goodness," Molly said.

"Actually, impersonally, it's too bad a few more people don't enjoy it." Dutch's words were slow, thought out.

171

"Remember, Yosemite is for the people, its owners, who should be aware of luring miles of quiet woods and pathless ridges, as well as great, public features like the Valley."

Tim teased, "Thank you, John Muir Vanderbunt."

"I wish we had brought a picnic dinner along," Molly sighed. "I'm not full of these trees yet, and they do feed my soul."

Swiftly, Dutch smiled at her, and she knew he shared her awed, mind-stretching feelings.

Tim skylarked, "To show you what a generous-hearted, forgiving fellow I am, we'll stop by the Lodge cafeteria and I'll treat all of you to dinner."

"But we're so dirty!" Molly made a face at her dusty, brush-clung clothes. "Let's go back to camp and change first."

"And you're the girl who doesn't care what other people think!" Tim exclaimed, half-seriously.

"At any rate, I have the answers to our common problem," Dutch said, walking toward his truck. "Along with my emergency supplies, I carry a whisk broom, soap, and a towel."

"After use of which," Tim concluded lightly, "we shall all appear neat, if not natty."

By the time they had retraced the rutty way to Yosemite Valley, enjoyed an uproarious meal, stopped for mail and gas it was nine-thirty when they pulled in the parking lot alongside Breck and Irving.

"Did you have a good day?" Breck questioned, leading them toward his tent.

Molly enthused. "I'm only sorry it has to end."

"It doesn't have to end yet!" Breck spoke jovially. "Does it, gang?"

At that, someone inside flung open the tent door, voices began singing "Happy birthday . . . ," Betty Fox appeared in the doorway with a candle-lit cake, and Foxy yelled *"Surprise!"* as he propelled Molly inside.

Astounded, she gazed first at the people seated beside, back of and on the picnic table; then at the cake lavishly decorated with pine cones and needles. Several times she opened her mouth to speak, then had to close it to swallow. Her eyes remained dry but chills chased her spine, and goose bumps pricked on her arms.

Behind her, Foxy chanted, "We didn't tell! She never even suspected anything when Dutch fiddled around so Dad and the other guys would be home from the talks. She didn't mention her birthday all day."

"I forgot it with all the other excitement." Her speech returned. "How did you know?"

Betty pleaded, "Please make a wish and blow out these candles before they expire."

Molly wrinkled her forehead, wishing fervently that she could express her thanks, blew mightily, and saw all twenty candles flame out.

"It's a lovely cake," she stated happily. "Who made it? Who decorated it so beautifully?"

From her crowded perch on the bed, Laura said, "I did. I took a cake decorating course in night school after baseball season was over last fall."

A shout of laughter went up. "I thank you," Molly said shyly, truthfully, "I don't deserve it." Painfully she remembered her rude rebuff of Laura's earlier kindness, of how she had ungraciously avoided the nightly camp get-togethers. "All this," she turned eloquent hands upward, "for me. It's not right."

Gloria smiled understandingly. "We just wanted an excuse to throw a real party."

"Yes," Betty backed her. "We were tired of coffee and cookies every night. Besides, the cake and ice cream are real Camp 19 efforts. I baked the cake."

"I supplied the eggs," Irving's wife said.

"We donated cream," Rowena added.

"Don't forget the cake of ice we bought," a naturalist teased. "It put me back twenty-five cents."

Breck turned to Dutch and Tim, who lounged by the door. "Thank them for keeping you away until after campfire talks."

In amazement, Molly asked, "Did you know too? How?"

"Foxy told us."

"And I confided in him," Betty scooped ice cream into bowls.

"And I was the sleuth behind the whole celebration," Gloria admitted. "Remember when you insisted you were venerable with years? You said, with great emphasis, that you were 'almost twenty.' "

Molly felt her cheeks warming, reddening.

"That claim clued me in, so one time when you were off on one of your famous, solitary rambles, I checked your driver's license for your birth date. Even if I hadn't done detective work, your mail today, which I brought home for you, would have told me. Two packages and several long, telltale birthday cards."

174

During all this, Molly's blush had spread to the roots of her hair, but her embarrassment wasn't the kind that made her want to disappear. All the eyes directed at her were friendly and understanding.

"Your day outdoors has certainly given you a sunburn," Betty teased. "Here are a couple of presents to add to your rosy glow."

Laura's gift wasn't a bit feminine. Molly was pleased speechless to unwrap copies of Thoreau's *Walden* and Muir's *Studies in the Sierra*. She smiled eloquent thanks; then tore open a bulky package from Gloria only to be freshly startled by a decidedly feminine pale yellow linen sheath. Her eyebrows rose.

Gloria said kindly, "It will add sophistication to your, shall we say, youthful wardrobe?"

The last package was accompanied by a funny card inscribed "From Camp 19 to its newest member," and held a new, lightweight backpack. "I bet Foxy told you mine has a hole in it and a broken strap." Molly was delighted. "Thank you all so much."

A glance at the card showed her Dutch's name in the long list. Along with many childish printings, there were some X's denoting camp babies. She resolved to mount the card in her naturalist notebook where it would remain a treasure forever.

The talk became general and lively with questions and elaborations about the Coulterville Road trip. Molly joined in occasionally and enjoyed the rest even though she was surrounded by people. Not just *people*, she realized, but Camp 19'ers, individuals who shared her love for Yosemite, and by their unselfish interests had

175

helped convert her from a loner to a contributing member of camp.

Without twisting around in her chair, she could not see Dutch; but when she did catch a glimpse of him, he looked relaxed and happy. When the party began to break up, he murmured in her ear, "I'll walk you home."

Molly's heart thudded. Did he suspect her feelings?

Carefully he placed her things on the tent stoop, saying, "Like to walk a bit?"

For the first time, he took her hand which slid naturally into his, and they strolled to the river's edge. Silently, darkly, it flowed along. A plopping splash marked a fish. A car hummed by back of them. Pine trees sighed before a breeze.

"Next to heaven, a river will suffice," Dutch said softly.

"Muir?"

"No, Molly girl. Don't confuse me with him. There are certain distinct similarities between our mountain-loving personalities, but John Muir and I are very different men."

"I'm glad you don't have a beard like his," Molly teased.

Dutch's words were low: "Do you suppose you could be a college professor's wife someday?"

Molly's heart was steady, her mind sure, but her answer, stopped by a kiss, wavered. "Yes, if his name is Amos Van. . ."